"My life," I amended q
Announce that you have no
Seriously, this is why you're
getting *my life* back."

I heard someone chuckle beside me, and I turned to see a gorgeous, six foot fridge-sized man smiling at me. He had short blond hair, stunning blue eyes, and he wore a gym uniform so tight it looked like it was painted on. He held out his hand, and I was almost scared to shake it in fear he would crush my fingers or something, but it was warm and firm. "My name's Reed. And you've come to the right place."

1 8 NOV 2024

2 2 NOV 2024

THE WEIGHT OF IT ALL

N.R. WALKER

COPYRIGHT

Cover Artist: N.R. Walker
Editor: Boho Edits
The Weight Of It All © 2016 N.R. Walker
Publisher: BlueHeart Press
Second Edition 2024

ALL RIGHTS RESERVED:

This literary work may not be reproduced or transmitted in any form or by any means, including electronic or photographic reproduction, in whole or in part, without express written permission.
This literary work may not be reproduced or transmitted in whole or in part in any form or by any means, including information storage and retrieval systems, or for use in AI training software.
This is a work of fiction, and any resemblance to persons, living or dead, or business establishments, events or locales is coincidental, except in the case of brief quotations embodied in critical articles and reviews. The Licensed Art Material is being used for illustrative purposes only.

WARNING:

Intended for an 18+ audience only. This book contains material that is intended for a mature, adult audience. It contains graphic language, explicit sexual content, and adult situations.

The author uses Australian English spelling and grammar.

TRADEMARKS:

All trademarks are the property of their respective owners.

Whenever you find
yourself doubting how
far you can go,
just remember how
far you have come.
Remember everything
you have faced,
all the battles
you have won,
and all the fears
you have overcome.

———

Unknown

N.R. WALKER

The Weight of it All

ONE

MOST PEOPLE CAN'T TELL YOU THE MOMENT THEIR life changed. One day they're twenty years old with the world at their feet, then the next they're closer to forty and wondering where the hell their life went. There's no *Logan's Run* age qualifier that deems you're past your use-by date. There's no ceremony with gowns and funny hats to say you've graduated from ticking one age-group box on a survey to ticking the next age-group box. You just turn around, and wham-bam-thank-you-very-fucking-much, you're old.

Well, old*er*.

I'm thirty-five. I don't classify myself as old. Well, I didn't.

Until Graham, my live-in boyfriend of eight years, came home and told me he was done. He didn't want to spend his life with an overweight old man. I wasn't fun anymore. I didn't look after myself anymore. I wasn't what he wanted.

And *that* was the moment my life changed.

Just to be clear on one thing, my now ex-boyfriend is the same age as me. And when he called me an old man, he wasn't having a dig at my age. He was having a go at how I lived my life. I didn't go out clubbing, I didn't go for runs through the park, I didn't want to go hiking on weekends.

Strolls for coffee, yes. And weekends at a log cabin reading books, doing wine tours, and cooking too much food, yes. I was more about enjoying the finer things in life, whereas he was avoiding his thirties the same way a cat avoided going to the vet. And apparently that made me old.

So the age comment I could ignore because I liked what I liked. But the overweight comment hit me hard.

After I'd gotten over the shock of his words and the shock of seeing his stuff packed in boxes and his front door key sitting on the kitchen bench, the realisation hit me that, yes, he really was leaving me. But the biggest shock came afterwards. After two bottles of wine and sobbing with my best friend, Anika, on the now-mostly-empty living room floor, I made my way to the bathroom. Drunk and an emotional mess, I stripped off intending to shower. Only I saw myself in the mirror and, for the first time, saw myself.

And I saw how Graham saw me, and I saw why he left me.

I was overweight. I did look old. I was a fucking mess.

So yes, that, the very lowest point of my life, was the day my life changed.

───────

Two days later I stood out the front of the local gym, which was ten minutes from my place, that I'd driven past a thousand times, gathering my resolve to walk inside. With a deep breath and newfound determination, I pushed through the doors and walked up to the reception counter. A young and fit looking woman smiled brightly at me. "Can I help you?"

"Yes. My name is Henry Beckett. And I need some help getting my boyfriend back."

She blinked. "Pardon?"

Two

Reed. Of course his name was Reed. He looked more like a Kelvin, as in Kelvinator——because he seriously was the size of a fridge——but I didn't say that out loud. He was what I imagined all gym junkies looked like: not an ounce of fat and beaming health and vitality. His skin was flawless, not overly tanned but in a my-diet-is-healthier-than-yours kind of way. His eyes were bright, his smile was friendly, his teeth perfectly straight. He could've been the guy on the "Benefits of Being Fit and Healthy" poster at the doctor's office I always rolled my eyes at.

"Come and take a seat," Reed said. He collected a clip-board off the counter and led the way over to one of the sofas in the waiting room. I had to wonder, what did a gym need a waiting room for? Did they serve coffee and cake here? I hoped they did, but given it was a gym, I didn't think so. It was cosy enough, even though the magazines on the coffee table were a mix of body building and cooking tasteless food.

I stared at the top magazine, my taste buds duly offended. "Have you ever eaten kale?" I asked. "It's hideous."

Reed grinned as he sat down. "It's not so bad."

"Sure. In the same way gastroenteritis isn't so bad," I said. "Or a fungal toenail infection."

He sat down, looking at me, clearly amused. "Not a fan, I take it?"

"Why eat something that is *not so bad*?" I asked. "I've always said life's too short for bad coffee, bad food, and bad s——" I counted these points off on my fingers but stopped short on number three, though from the way Reed smiled at the clipboard, I'm pretty sure he knew what *S* word I was referring to. "Shoes," I finished lamely. Though now that I thought about it, good shoes were just as enjoyable as good sex.

God, I really am an old man.

I sat down on the sofa with a kerplunk and a sigh. Reed let the clipboard sit on his lap, and he looked at me worriedly and frowned. "Who's Graham?"

"What?"

He put his hand up like he was stopping traffic. "You *just* said, 'And that's why Graham left me.'"

Oh shit. Did I? "Graham... Graham is the new Voldemort. We don't speak his name out loud anymore."

Reed's look of worry was soon a smile. "Oh." He nodded sagely. "And this is the Voldemort you want back?"

"No. Yes. Well, maybe. It'll take more than gathering up a few Horcruxes, I'm afraid. Unless you can call running on a treadmill a Horcrux."

Reed blinked slowly. "A what?"

"A Horcrux. You know, from *Harry Potter*?"

He looked genuinely surprised. "I've never actually seen the movies or read the books. Though I know who Voldemort is."

I stared at him then leaned in like it was top secret. My voice was just a whisper. "So, you're the one?"

"I'm the one what?"

"The one person on the planet who hasn't seen the movies or read the books."

Reed laughed this time. "Yes, that would be me." Still smiling, he held up the clipboard. "Some questions for you."

I leaned back and sighed. "Does this include a waiver in case I drop dead on the StairMaster? Because, just so you know, it probably should because I probably will."

He chuckled just as the lady behind the counter called his name and held up the phone receiver. He looked at me apologetically. "Sorry, but I better take that call. How about you fill in the details, and I'll come back when you're done?"

"Sure," I said, taking the clipboard. The first questions were the usual: name, address, occupation, private health cover details. I considered drawing a little hand with its middle finger extended next to the age bracket box but figured it probably wasn't appropriately mature next to the 35-40 box. I mean really, would it have killed them to have the selection criteria as 30-35? Why did the 35s need to be grouped with the 40s?

Right about then, I could've killed Anika. When I told her, my best friend since college, that I was going to join a gym, she told me that Graham was a jerk and I didn't need to change one thing about me. But when she realised I was adamant about losing weight, she was most encouraging. Told me it was an excellent idea! When I asked her to come and join with me, she simply patted my hand and told me not to be a fucking idiot. I considered putting the form down and bailing out. I could be home with a bottle of wine and some Greek food in twenty minutes, wallowing in my own loneliness, telling Anika over the phone about my harrowingly close call with a gym.

But then what would I achieve? I didn't want to be the overweight drunk guy crying in my bathroom ever again.

So with a deep breath, I filled out the rest of the form.

There were other questions like allergies and other sports-related injuries, which made me snort because they assumed I'd actually done some kind of sport in my life.

"What's so funny?" Reed asked. He was now standing in front of where I sat, obviously finished with his phone call.

He was so tall, I had to crane my neck to look at him, and I briefly considered writing down that as an injury. "Well, sports-related injuries would imply partaking in some kind of physical activity. The only marathons I've done are *Game of Thrones* and *Breaking Bad* marathons." Then I remembered another one. "Oh, and *Sex and the City*, but I was sick that week, so it doesn't count."

This time, he sat down beside me. "You're really funny."

"Well, I tend to talk a lot. When I'm not at work, that is. You know that song 'the knee bone's connected to the what-ever bone'?" He nodded and I sighed. "Well, my mouth isn't connected to my brain."

"No filter?"

I shook my head. "Birth defect. Suffered from it all my life."

He tried not to laugh and took the clipboard. "Okay, you ready for a quick physical?"

I blanched. "Like now? Today? Here? With you? Ugh, do I have to be there?"

His grin was wide and perfect. "Kinda helps if you are, yeah." He stood up and waited for me to follow. "Come on, this way."

I reluctantly followed him into what I thought was an office, but as it turned out, it was some kind of torture chamber. There were weighing scales, and a "Healthy Eating Pyramid" chart on the wall. I'm sure if I went through the desk drawer, there'd be horrendously cruel implements like measuring tapes and fat pinchers.

"No need to look so scared," he said, sliding the clipboard onto the table.

"Has anyone died in here?"

Reed barked out a laugh. "Not to my knowledge."

"Or just people's hopes and dreams?"

His shoulders shook as he laughed. "And the souls of small children."

I nodded. "Sounds about right."

His eyes were warm, matching his Colgate smile. "Okay, height first," he said, nodding toward the chart on the wall. He levelled off the top of my head with his pen and wrote down his findings. Not that I expected my height to change a great deal. "Five-ten," he confirmed. He collected a tape measure from the desk drawer and, clearly not having any personal space issues, measured my chest, waist, each thigh, and each bicep.

"Last time I got measured was for my sister's wedding," I said as he did his measure-and-write thing. "Couldn't tell you what the measurements were."

"How long ago was that?" he asked. "The wedding?"

"Three years ago."

"Nice," he said politely.

"Hmm, maybe. The suit lasted longer than the marriage though. Clearly I got the better deal."

He balked. "Oh. Sorry."

I snorted. "Don't sweat it. She's been engaged to someone else since then too but freaked out before the wedding. She's latched onto some other poor guy now." I shook my head. I loved my sister, but she treated marriage like interior decorating and changed with the seasons. Gay and lesbian people weren't afforded the same luxury in this country, and it was a sore point for me. If Graham and I could've had the wedding we'd once wanted... then I remembered I didn't have a Graham anymore.

"Hop up onto the scales for me?" Reed asked. He obviously wasn't privy to the nosedive in my thoughts and mood. With a reluctant and somewhat petulant sigh, I did as he asked. "Then we'll take a photo for your 'before' picture, and when you reach your goal weight or the fitness level you'd like to achieve, we can take an 'after' picture."

I heard what he said, but I was stuck staring at the numbers on the scale. Surely they were wrong. Could digital scales even be wrong?

Reed's voice was soft beside me. "You okay?"

I was speechless and horrified and embarrassed. "Holy shit," I whispered.

One hundred and fourteen kilos.

Triple figures. One hundred and fourteen fucking kilos.

I stepped back off the scales, feeling light-headed and dazed. I'd never been this weight. I think the last time I weighed myself was about ten years ago, and I was eighty-five kilos. How the fuck was I one hundred and fourteen kilos? And the worst part, was that Graham was right. I was overweight. I'd let myself go. I stopped taking care of myself.

"Fuck."

Reed put his hand on my arm. "Like I said, Henry, you're in the right place. We'll get some goals written up, a workout plan, a diet plan. You'll get your life back. And your boyfriend. We'll have you looking so damn good, he'll be begging you to take him back."

I nodded numbly. I was truly in shock. I had no witty comeback. I had nothing funny to say.

Reed gave me a pitying, reassuring smile. He snapped my photo for his stupid before picture, and all I could think of was *one hundred and fourteen kilos*.

He stood in front of me and put his huge hands on my shoulders. "Henry, look at me."

I blinked rapidly and tried to shake off my shame. I looked

him right in his pretty eyes, feeling every part of *Beauty and the* Obese *Beast*. "Is this where you sing 'A Tale As Old As Time' and I give you a library?"

He quirked an eyebrow and fought a smile. "What?"

"Never mind."

"You can do everything I set out for you, and I'll be with you every step of the way," he said. "You've got this."

He told me to be there at eight in the morning, ready to change my outlook, ready to change my life.

I went home in a daze. I considered calling Anika, but she'd only tell me I was perfect the way I was, and one hundred and fourteen fucking kilos begged to differ. So instead, I ate the remaining leftover cheesecake from the fridge, and cried.

THREE

BEING AT THE GYM AT EIGHT IN THE MORNING ON A Sunday was ridiculous. The fact that some people were finishing up from an hour session already was even crazier. Did these perfect people sleep? And realistically, that meant they must have gotten here sometime after six to be here to start at seven. To exercise. On a Sunday, the day where I normally slept in and went out for a lazy brunch. But exercising? I had concerns for their psychological well-being.

"Hey, Henry!" Reed greeted me cheerfully. "So glad you're here."

I watched two women as they left, all sweaty and laughing. "Do you do psych evals or blot tests on these people?" I asked Reed quietly. "Because I think they might have some mental health concerns."

Reed threw his head back and laughed. "Oh, you crack me up." He seemed genuinely happy, and given he'd been here, probably working out since six himself, made me question his sanity.

"So do you have to be crazy to do exercise for a living?"

He grinned. "Nope. But it helps." He clapped his hands

together. "I've worked out an exercise and diet plan for you." He collected some sheets of paper and showed me the exercise plan first. "Cardio, core training, and body strength will be the main focuses of the first four weeks. We'll start slow and work our way up, okay?"

I nodded bleakly.

"And the diet plan is fairly broad. You said food is your thing, so it's important to get this side right just as much as the exercise, because if this doesn't work for you, then you'll be more likely to quit."

"Does it include kale?"

He grinned. "No kale."

"Good."

"Come on and I'll show you what I've got planned for you." He walked with a bounce in his step over to a row of treadmills.

I did my best David Attenborough impersonation. "Ah, modern, yet archaic torture devices in their natural habitat. Not a particularly threatening species unless you're an over-weight thirty-five year old who hasn't run since high school." Then I remembered that wasn't exactly true. "Okay, well, running to grab a half-priced KitchenAid in the Boxing Day sales doesn't count."

Reed was staring at me, still smiling. "Did you get it?"

"Get what?"

"The KitchenAid."

"Oh, of course. I love to cook. It's my thing. And there was no chef or grandma alive brave enough to get in the road of a man on a mission. Although I still do feel bad about elbowing that lady. She was faster than me; she wore running shoes, and I wore my Diesel loafers. Style over comfort, you know how that is. But let me tell you, I never made that mistake on a sale day again." Reed looked at me for a long moment, like I baffled and amused him in equal measure.

"Sorry. I tend to talk a lot. Not a great deal of it makes sense."

His grin was slow-spreading but genuine. "Makes perfect sense to me. Okay, we'll start with some cardio." Then he pressed some buttons on the treadmill. "I'm gonna set this for you. See this?" He pressed some more buttons while I watched. "It'll start with a slow-but-steady walk, then it'll get a little faster, incline a little like you're walking uphill, then it'll slow back down to your starting pace." I stepped onto the machine, and he hit the start button. "I'll be back when you're done, okay?"

He left me to it, walking over to some other fit-looking gym members, giving them the exact amount of attentive and professional time he gave me. He was good at his job. Definitely a people person, and the way everyone called him by name and him them, I assumed he was well-liked.

I watched him while he spoke to a lady who was using some arm-pulling torture device and then helped a guy lifting weights. He looked over at me every so often and smiled as I huffed and puffed my way through what he'd called a gentle stroll. Jesus, if I walked this gently anywhere, I'm sure I'd be dead before I got there.

Then holy shit, the treadmill beeped and started to tilt. The platform rose up, and sweet mother of God, I was going to die.

After I got used to the change, Reed was beside me. "Looking good," he said, his usual smile firmly in place.

I fully intended to reply with some intelligent and witty comeback, but walking up a non-existent hill for five minutes left me incapable of breathing and talking at the same time.

I thought about hitting the stop button. Actually, pressing that emergency stop button in hopes that an ambulance would arrive and drive me to the nearest coffee shop was very tempting.

But I knew if I started making excuses now, I was wasting everyone's time and proving Graham right. And that's what made me push through it. Sure enough, after an eternity in hell, the treadmill declined and the pace slowed.

When it came to a stop, I hopped off. My legs were absolute jelly, my lungs burned, and my heart was nearing cardio-fatal levels.

Reed clapped his huge hand on my back. "How was that?"

I held my hand up, still too out of breath to speak. So I nodded instead and managed a few one-syllable words. "Not. Good. Exer. Cise. Bad."

He laughed again. "You pushed through it. You did really well."

I nodded and wiped my face down with my towel. "Yeah. That was great," I managed to say. "Thanks. See you tomorrow?"

Reed fought a smile. "Uh, that was just your warm up."

God help me. "Well," I panted. "Consider me sufficiently warmed up. Overly warmed, actually. Hot, if I'm being honest. I think I'm going to expire. As in, drop dead." I walked, somewhat shakily, over to the closest weight bench and sat on it. My heart was still trying to kill me. My lungs felt like they were fighting for room in my chest.

Reed clapped his huge hand on my shoulder. He was really rather touchy-feely. "Come on, on your feet. You've got more in you yet."

I put my hand up, still trying to catch my breath. "One sec. My lungs are broken."

He snorted out a laugh. "Come on, get up."

Somehow, I stood. Reed took me over to a StairMaster machine. "Oh, I've seen these in action before," I said. "In Hugo's House of Pain, except the guy was strapped on and he was naked and——" Reed's eyes went wide. "——and that was a long time ago. I'm not into leather; it was just one night. Sorry, what were you saying?"

Reed slow-blinked then started to laugh. It took him a moment to stop laughing, not that I minded because the longer he laughed at me, the less time I was gonna be on that exercise machine.

Still smiling, he shook his head. "Okay, step up on it for me."

I did that.

"Hold onto the handles," he said. I did that, and he continued to explain, "The elliptical is a cross-trainer. You will use lower body and upper body. It's great for cardio, similar to the treadmill but with no impact." He rattled off the physical benefits, to which I simply nodded and smiled——in a slightly horrified kind of way——then he went through the settings on screen and set it for two minutes. "Just a short one today. I just want you to get a feel for it. You ready?"

"Not at all."

He chuckled and hit start. Fuck. It was like climbing stairs while holding ski stocks or two Gandalf staffs. *Thou shall not pass* was too bloody right. I'd never make it in Middle Earth because two minutes on this frickin' machine almost killed me. Fuck going to Mordor. I couldn't even go around the block.

The machine finally slowed, and I stepped off. My legs were past the consistency of jelly and were more of a slush, and my lungs were on fire. I was surprised I wasn't breathing out smoke.

Reed saw that I was finished and came back over to me, his smile wide. "How was that?"

I put my hands on my knees. I mean sure, I was out of breath, but if I didn't hold my knees, I'm certain my legs would've buckled. "I'm sure this violates the Geneva Convention."

Reed's smile became a grin. "You're really funny."

I stared at him. "I'm being serious." I stood up straight and my heart, lungs, and ribs protested. "Ugh. Jesus Christ. And this is supposed to be good for me?"

"You're doing great," he said quietly. "First time's never easy."

"Yeah. That's what he said."

He stared at me, then barked out a laugh. "I see what you mean about the no filter."

I waved my hand at him, still trying not to die of aerobic asphyxiation. I took as deep a breath as my lungs would allow, then another, until I was somewhat sure I was going to live. And I had to do this. If I wanted my life back, I had to quit bitching and get it done. "Okay, so what other torture devices are there?"

Reed grinned victoriously. "Over here." He led me to some metal frame contraption that had cables and pulleys. "This is called a cable and pulley machine."

"The person who invented it didn't have an extensive vocabulary, did they? Or an imagination."

His warm smile matched his eyes, but he ignored my comment. "This is for the strength part of your workout program. Stand here like this," he said, standing under the frame. He held the two separate handgrips and proceeded to pull them back and forward effortlessly; his arms and shoulders bulged and flexed with each movement. He then went on to do a range of different positions and exercises, telling me which muscles benefited from each one. "The weight is set at forty kilos, but that's what's good about this machine. You can set the weight to suit anyone. What do you think you can lift?"

I tried to do the maths based on full martini glasses, because I lift those without any problem, but Reed changed the weight to ten kilos before I got done counting.

"We'll start you off light. I really just want you to get the technical aspect down pat first. To make sure you're using the equipment correctly so you don't injure yourself when you work out when I'm not here." Reed moved to the side, giving me room to take his place. "Okay, your turn."

I did as he did, then somehow managed to get through everything he told me to do, using muscles I hadn't used in... well, ever. He put his huge hand on different parts of my body as I did the different movements. Biceps, triceps, pecs, deltoids, lats. Then he showed me proper stretching techniques, doing each one with me.

I was on the floor with one leg underneath me, the other bent behind me, apparently stretching my quads but really just looking like an overweight pretzel. "Oh God, this is going to hurt tomorrow."

He gave me a sympathetic smile. "Yes, it will. And the day after will probably be worse. But you'll get better every time, and in a week or two, you'll be fine."

"I have to work tomorrow," I admitted, trying not to sound like a whiney baby. "And I can't turn up at the office and not be able to move."

"What exactly does a financial actuary for one of the country's biggest banks do?"

Oh, so he read my personal information sheet I filled out yesterday. "I study statistics and trends to manage potential risks."

He blinked. "Potential risks?"

I nodded. "Yes. I evaluate the likelihood of future events that would impact our industry."

Reed made a thoughtful face. "Interesting."

"You're the first person I've ever met to call it that."

"Really?"

"Most people think it's boring, but I actually enjoy it. I like numbers. They're constant, and the answers are invariable."

"Even in a hypothetical event that may or may not happen?"

Now it was me who stared at him. My God, he understood what I did? "Yes, even then."

He nodded slowly as a smile played at his lips. "I like that."

"You like numbers?"

"Maths was always my favourite subject at school," he answered. "Well, sport, then maths."

"I hated sport."

He smiled. "Well, you did great today. Nailed the equipment. Did you have a chance to look over the diet plan I gave you?"

"Yeah. I intended to go shopping later today, but I think I might just go home and die first. I'm already starting to feel sore." I rotated my shoulder and regretted it immediately. "Ow."

He grimaced. "Yeah, you're going to be sore. But, and this is only a suggestion... go shopping before you get home. Once you get home, showered, and sitting down, the very last thing you'll feel like doing is grocery shopping." Then he added brightly, "Plus, you can get some Epsom salts or another muscle soak. Have you got a bath at home?"

"Yes." Though I couldn't remember the last time I'd actually had a bath.

"It will help. A hot bath with magnesium salts and a drop or two of lavender right before bed, and you'll sleep like a baby."

I reluctantly agreed. "Anything that helps has to be a good thing, I guess."

Reed's perfect smile beamed. "Excellent. So, take it easy tomorrow. Do the stretches I showed you and some gentle walking, and that will help. I promise you, Henry, if you do three sessions a week, by the end of next week, you'll see and feel the difference. I'm not going to lie to you: it's not going to be easy. You will hurt; you will want to never come back. But you *will* come back. You want this, and you can do this."

I nodded. "Yeah, okay."

His smile died and his brow furrowed. "You okay?"

"Yeah, why?"

"No snarky comment."

"That's just because I've gone into an exercise-induced shock. Loss of humour is the first sign of impending death."

He gave me a weak smile and gently clapped my shoulder. "I will see you the day after tomorrow, yeah? 7:00 a.m."

I nodded and winced. "Nodding hurts, so can I give one blink for yes and two blinks for no? I'm pretty sure my eyelids don't hurt, though it's highly likely I feel so sore, my brain has sent out neural blocks and I can no longer feel pain."

He laughed again, just as someone called his name. He checked his watch, told me he'd see me next time, and went off to see his other clients. I limped to my car and set about driving to the nearest Coles. I tried not to think about the pain, lamely telling myself I was changing my life for the better. And that worked just fine and dandy until I actually had to get out of the car and walk into the supermarket.

Oh Lord baby Jesus in a manger. Stiff and sore already, I gingerly collected all the fruit and vegetables on my list. I deliberately didn't look at the deli section, knowing those antipasto goodies would never pass my lips again. I said a quiet farewell to the cheese section, also never again to be enjoyed with a glass of wine on Sunday afternoons.

I always served cheese with fig pastes and crackers and wine on Sunday afternoons for Graham and I...

Not that it mattered. I couldn't have cheese or wine, and I had no Graham. A sob escaped me in the refrigerated aisle of Coles. I'm pretty sure it was the cold reality of Graham leaving me that stripped my emotions raw... Or maybe it was the loss of wine and cheese, or how my body hurt so much. It was kind of hard to tell.

A lady put her hand on my arm; concern clouded her face. "Are you okay, love?"

I tried to communicate by blinking twice. Which meant no, but she mustn't have been fluent. So instead I had to speak. "I've just been to my first ever gym session, and I think I broke my body. I have some stupid diet plan, so I can't have wine or bacon, and all because my boyfriend of eight years left me."

She slow-blinked twice. Oh good, she was fluent in blink-speak.

"Yes, he did. He said it's because I'm overweight."

She blinked once.

Did she just agree with me? "Do you think I'm fat?" *How rude!*

"Pardon?"

"Can you communicate by blinking?"

Someone behind me laughed, and I turned to find Reed, looking taller than I remembered, holding a shopping basket and grinning that perfect smile. He stepped over to me and gave the lady a sympathetic nod. "It's okay," he said to her. "I'll take it from here."

We watched as she hurried away. "I don't think she speaks in blinks," I explained.

Reed chuckled again, but his eyes softened. "Are you okay?"

"No. My body has seized up. I'm pretty sure there was an old guy back in the dairy section in one of those motorised scooters. If you could just go push him out of it and tell him there's someone much more in need of it in aisle two."

Reed laughed. "No, I certainly will not." Then he shoved the basket handle up to the crook of his elbow, put his two huge hands on my shoulders, and gently pushed. "Walk. This way."

"Ow, ow, ow," I said with each step, which of course made him laugh. He never took his hands off me and pushed me all the way to aisle six. "If you even think about telling me there's no gain without pain, I'll shove this eggplant right where the sun doesn't shine."

"Only if you wash it first and use a lot of lube." Stunned, I tripped over my feet, but he caught me. "I'm kidding," he said with a laugh, still pushing me along.

By the time my brain had caught up to the fact that Reed had joked about arseplay, we were in the Personals aisle. We went past the condoms and lube, and he just happened to stop pushing me in front of the strapping tape, muscle rubs, and Band-Aids. "Here," he declared, plucking a box off the bottom shelf. "Epsom salts. Take a hot bath with this. It will help."

I took the offered box. "An eggplant? Really?"

Reed threw his head back and laughed. "I was joking!"

"I should hope so. I mean, a carrot or cucumber maybe, but an eggplant is a little ambitious."

He fought a smile. "When I gave you the diet plan that insisted on a range of vegetables, that wasn't what I really had in mind."

I smiled at him, glad he played along. Not everyone thought my random trains of thought and subsequent ramblings were entertaining. Graham was used to the drivel that came out of my mouth. Actually, he'd stopped his own quips back over the years, and if I were being honest, he'd ignored most things I talked about.

"You okay?" Reed asked. He was staring at me, concerned and a little sad.

"Yeah, sorry. Just remembering something."

"From your ex?"

I nodded and regretted it immediately. "Ouch. Nodding hurts. Can we converse in blinks?"

He blinked once. *Yes.*

I laughed then tried to bend down to grab something off the shelf and yelped. My whole body was frozen and stuck. "Oh, good Lord. I'm pretty sure I'm going to die."

Reed put his hand on my shoulder and helped me stand upright. He frowned sympathetically. "Henry, will you be okay?"

I blinked once, for yes. Then blinked again, for no.

"Got your phone on you?"

"Yeah." I slowly fished my phone out of my pocket, withholding the urge to groan as my muscles objected. "Why do you ask?"

He took it out of my hand and proceeded to thumb in some numbers and hit Send. A moment later, his phone buzzed somewhere on his body. "You now have my number," he said, typing something into my phone. He handed it back to me, and I saw that he'd added his name and number into my Contacts.

Reed Henske.

"Just in case you need to speak to someone," he said. His usual confident demeanour was gone. Now he seemed unsure. "About things like how sore is normal tomorrow and what pain isn't normal."

"I'm pretty sure none of it is normal."

"And now I have your number, I can make sure you come back to the gym the day after tomorrow."

"If I haven't died of extreme muscle fatigue." Oh Jesus. "Can someone actually die of muscle fatigue?"

Reed chuckled. "You're not going to die. Come on, I'll help you through checkout."

"Have you got everything?" I asked. His shopping basket only had a twelve pack of eggs in it.

"I just need to go to the deli."

He turned to walk in that direction and I tried to go with him, but the best I could do was a rusted Tin Man impersonation. "Oh, sweet Lord have mercy."

Reed tried not to laugh. "You poor thing."

"It's your fault."

He scoffed. "You'll be thanking me in a few weeks."

"I'd thank you right now if you find that old guy in that motorised scooter." He refused to toss the old guy out of his scooter for me, but he did smile a lot. We walked——well, he walked and I shuffled——over to the deli where he ordered chicken and fish fillets. I grabbed some meat and fish too, ignoring the cheese and antipasto deliciousness, and then we walked/hobbled to the checkout.

"You live close by?" I asked as we waited in line. "Well, I presume this supermarket is either between work and home or close by."

"Yep. I live not far from here."

"Me too," I admitted. "Do you always work on Sundays?"

"Six till ten." He started loading my groceries onto the conveyor belt at the checkout. "It's good. I get to work out, help other people work out, earn money while I'm doing it, and be done by mid-morning. The rest of my day is free."

He finished putting my items onto the checkout then proceeded to fill the trolley again with the bagged items. He was doing it all for me as he talked about having days off during the week in lieu of working weekends, but if someone couldn't do a shift, he'd usually do it for them. He obviously loved what he did. I couldn't deny looking at the muscles in his biceps and triceps flex as he leaned and lifted. I wasn't actively looking, but I wasn't fucking dead either.

I paid for my groceries and waited for Reed to pay for his few things, and we walked out together. Well, he walked and I staggered/leaned on the trolley for support, all the way to my car. I popped the boot. "Nice," he said, nodding approvingly at my car.

"Thanks." My Audi TT was nice. I loved it. I worked hard for my salary and splurged on myself to buy the car of my dreams. Then I groaned as I lifted a bag into the boot. "God I'm gonna die trying to go to work tomorrow."

He gently put his hand on my arm. "You have my number. Call or text me if you need." Then he started to walk to the edge of the car park. "See you on Tuesday."

I called out after him. "Are you walking?"

"Yep."

"Need a lift?"

"Nah, I'm good."

I waved Reed off and lowered myself agonizingly into my car and watched him as he walked up the tree-lined street away from the car park. The area was filled with newish apartment blocks, and he crossed the street and walked to the end of the road before disappearing from view. I wasn't really sitting there for five minutes watching him, I told myself. I only watched him because I was unable to move, I conceded, my muscles cramped and frozen. When he was long gone, I started the car, never more thankful for the automatic transmission, and went home.

I struggled to get the bags inside to the kitchen, taking each step with a groan. Sure, I felt productive and even a little energised for doing exercise. I'd taken the first step in changing my life. So, I kinda felt good for that, but sweet mother of God, my body, from head to toe, hurt like hell.

FOUR

PAIN WOKE ME UP IN THE MIDDLE OF THE NIGHT. I must've tried to roll over and my muscles protested loudly. Still half-asleep, I tapped the other side of the bed, trying to wake Graham. It wasn't until my hand found nothing but cold sheets that I remembered Graham was no longer here. My heart ached along with the rest of my body, so it was kind of fitting, I guess.

I very gingerly got out of bed, letting out a long "owwwww" as I stood. Making my way to the bathroom like a ninety year old, I popped some Advil and very deliberately didn't look at myself in the mirror. I couldn't deal with how pathetic I felt. I didn't need to see it in front of me.

My whole body hurt. My legs, arms, chest, back, everywhere. I shuffled back to bed, still surprised to see it empty, Graham's side unslept in, and felt the pang of longing and loneliness in my heart intensify that made all my other aches and pains seem insignificant.

. . .

I WAS awake before my alarm, staring at the ceiling and trying not to move. I didn't even have to move to know what hurt. Everything hurt without trying. Today was going to be hell. I had no way of knowing if soaking in the bath last night helped at all, and I had to wonder how I would've felt if Reed hadn't told me to do it. But knowing that moving and gently stretching out the muscles, along with a hot shower, would help, I made myself get up.

"Jesus Herbert Christ."

I groaned loudly with each step to the bathroom. And if I thought for one minute I was sore yesterday, today was a whole new level of pain. Reaching for the shower taps hurt, the hot water hurt, trying to wash my body hurt, drying off hurt, getting dressed hurt. Putting on shoes and doing up my laces was a feat worthy of the Masochist Olympics.

Everything hurt. Every fucking thing.

I washed some Panadol down with my coffee and somehow managed to drive to work. I walked like I wore razor wire underwear. People eyed me weirdly, but I was always quiet at work, more reserved, so no one in the foyer really spoke to me. I mean, I'd worked there for six years under the chief actuary, and somehow managed to engage my brain/mouth filter, or rarely did I speak at all. It was safer that way. I think most people thought I was unapproachable or cranky even, but it allowed for a professional distance which was for the best really.

The only person who was accustomed to my verbal diarrhoea was my personal assistant, Melinda Chen. She was a young mathematical wiz, the eldest daughter to Chinese parents, with a brilliant mind for detail. She had shoulder-length, straight black hair, John-Lennon-style glasses, a penchant for Korean pop music, and Japanese comic books. She knew I was gay, never batted an eyelid, and knew I was very recently single. I'd been a shell-shocked zombie last

Thursday and Friday after my disastrous initiation back into singledom. Apparently I looked a lot worse today.

She took one look at me, the papers in her hand forgotten. "What the hell happened to you?"

"It's a long story." I shuffled past her into my office and lowered myself slowly, painfully, into my desk chair. "Shut the door?"

She did as I asked and sat across from me. Her concern was clear on her face. "Are you okay?"

I shook my head. "No, not really. Graham left me."

She frowned, but there was confusion in her eyes. "Yes, I know."

"Told me I was fat, basically."

Melinda's nostrils flared. "Well, if that's how he treats you after eight years together, then good riddance, I say."

Did I mention she had the tact of a bull in a china shop? "That's not the reason I feel like I've been hit by a bus."

She brightened. "Did you go out and hook up? Two days of sex is quite a workout."

"What? No!"

"Oh."

"I joined a gym. I have a personal trainer."

"You what?!"

"I know."

"Did you lose your mind?"

"I think so. And my dignity. And my ability to move without excruciating pain."

"I'll pick something up for you," she said with a nod. "Coffee first?"

"Yes, please." Then I thought better of it. "Just one sugar. I'm cutting back."

She grimaced. "Ouch."

"You have no idea."

"The Gallagher reports are on your desk," she said,

nodding to the pile of folders that weren't there on Friday afternoon when I'd left.

I nodded and everything seized up. "Nodding hurts."

"We can communicate by blinking if you'd prefer."

"Oh my God, you are my twin soul. Thank you."

"I was kidding."

"Oh."

But then, because she knew me so well, she said, "What's the code?"

"One blink for yes. Two blinks for no."

She stood up. "Okay. I'll be back."

I blinked once so she'd know her statement was received and understood, and she smiled before walking out and softly closing the door behind her.

I went to take the top folder from the pile and realised, very abruptly, that my arms wouldn't work. My wrists kinda stuck out at ninety-degree angles from my sides because apparently my shoulders, biceps, and triceps were on strike.

Melinda came back with my coffee and put it on my desk at my right. I flapped my useless hand at it, but actually reaching it involved using muscles that didn't want to be used.

Melinda stared at me and my pathetic attempt to move. "Is that your best T-Rex impersonation?"

I blinked once and she laughed.

God, it was going to be a long day.

AFTER A FEW HOURS of going through the job files, thankful I didn't have to move much, I'd almost forgotten my body hated me until I tried to stand up.

And holy crap, everything was worse. And really fucking sore. "Ow, ow, ow."

Before I could fall back into my chair and die, my phone

buzzed. I looked at the screen, and was surprised to see Reed's name. I hit Answer, then Speaker. "Hello?"

"Hi, it's Reed, from the gym." He cleared his throat. "Sorry for calling you at work. Hope that's okay. Just calling to see how you're doing?"

"Oh my God, I'm dying."

"I'm sure it's not quite that bad——"

"I think there's a high chance I could have SPS, which is a rare disease but not unheard of."

"SPS?"

"Stiff Person Syndrome."

He laughed.

"Don't laugh, it's a real disease. Real people suffer from it. I think I could be suffering from it. Either that, or possibly Lyme's Disease. Or Chronic Exertional Compartment Syndrome. Or claudication."

"You Googled muscle soreness, didn't you?"

I pouted. "Maybe."

He laughed again, but it was a warm, soft sound. "Henry, you're not dying. What you're experiencing is called 'delayed onset muscle soreness,' and it's completely normal."

"Well, I'm stuck in a standing position at my desk, and my PA thinks I look like a T-Rex because my arms can't extend all the way out."

Now he laughed louder. "Well, your sense of humour is still fully functional."

"Oh great, so my cause of death will read, "Died a horrible painful death from a broken body. Sense of humour still fully functional."

"You're not going to die. Well, not today from muscle soreness."

"Oh gee, thanks."

"Do you want to come in this afternoon and I can take you through some gentle stretching exercises?"

I sighed. "No. Ignore me. I'm prone to over-exaggeration. And maybe a touch of melodrama. And it's quite possible I can be a bit of a drama queen. Or so I'm told." I rolled my eyes hard at that, surprised that didn't hurt. "I'm sure I'll be okay."

There was a soft huff on the other end of the phone, and I could just imagine him smiling. "Keep moving. Walk around your office if you can, just slowly."

"Slowly?" I cried. "I'm sure there are folks in their nineties who can walk faster than me right now."

"Just keep moving," he said again. I could tell he was smiling now. "It will help. Nothing too strenuous, just enough to get you through work. Then rest tonight when you get home, and take another bath with Epsom salts before you go to bed."

"And tomorrow?"

"Tomorrow I'll see you back here at 7:00 a.m."

I groaned, maybe even cried a little.

"Henry, you'll be fine. You're doing the right thing. You'll be better for it, I promise you."

My desk phone rang. "I have to go," I said to Reed.

"You'll be here tomorrow?"

I considered saying no. I considered going home and eating an entire pizza just to teach him a lesson. But then I knew I was only cheating myself, and worse, proving Graham right. "Yes, I'll be there at seven."

"Good man. See you then."

I disconnected the call to Reed and answered my work phone. My attention was drawn to accounts, reports, and deadlines, and the distraction was welcome.

I did as Reed suggested: kept moving, just slowly, but moving all the same. And Reed was right, moving was key. Because when I stopped for lunch, it was awfully hard to move again. I sat in my usual corner of the lunchbreak room, reading the latest celeb magazine on my phone when I went to stand, only stopping halfway with a strangled cry.

Melinda was suddenly beside me. "Stand up straight, nice and slow," she instructed quietly, so no one else in the room would hear. "We're gonna walk out of here together, and you're gonna push through the pain, okay?"

I blinked once for yes and she smiled. Melinda knew I hated showing any signs of weakness in front of other staff members. I was second in charge of my division, and there was a long line of people who were vying to climb the ladder, just waiting for me to stumble, professionally speaking. Literally speaking would just be embarrassing all round, and I certainly didn't want to give any of them anything to laugh at me over.

It was a personal hang up of mine, having people laugh at me. I knew that, and thankfully, so did Melinda.

I blinked once. She took my lunch container for me, and I somehow managed to walk out of the lunchbreak room without making an arse of myself. Once in my office, I lowered my sore old body into my desk chair. "Thank you."

"You're welcome." She put my lunch container on my desk and stared at what was left of my salad like it was rotten chicken gizzards. "That's disgusting."

"Rocket salad with sundried tomatoes and brown rice, feta, and French salad dressing," I explained. "It was on some healthy eating recipe blog."

"Oh God." She looked horrified. "They've possessed you and brainwashed you. Exercising *and* dieting. Next thing you know you'll be saying it was actually palatable."

"It actually wasn't that bad."

She stared at me, unblinking.

"Thank you for helping me out back there."

"Mmm." Melinda was now studying me like I was speaking in tongues. "No problem. Oh, and I got you these."

She pulled a white paper bag from her satchel and handed it to me.

"Is it some traditional Chinese remedy from your grandmother?"

Melinda rolled her eyes. "Jesus Henry, do I look like the *Karate Kid* to you?"

"Sorry."

"I got it from the chemist on York. You know when you say to the pharmacist 'my boss decided to go break himself doing exercise and now he can't move'? Well, that's what she gave me to give you."

"Thank you."

"You're welcome." She walked to the door. "I'll have the Juniper reports done by this afternoon."

"You're worth more money."

"Then pay me more money."

I laughed a sarcastic laugh, which she mimicked perfectly before walking out the door. The pharmacist had given me magnesium tablets and multivitamins and Advil. I swallowed down two of each and prayed for immediate relief.

———

I SPENT the afternoon studying the stock market and data analytics, as well as reports on energy resources and the environment, while walking slowly around my office, and the only time I sat for any length of time was for a teleconference with the other head office in Melbourne. My boss, a lady by the name of Lillian Caldwell, was in Singapore all week, and that left me signing off on reports in her absence. I would be doing longer hours this week which, in hindsight, probably wasn't the best timing to have a midlife crisis.

Thanks a fucking lot, Graham.

I was still sore as hell, and I'd never been happier to see six o'clock. Melinda had left a little after five, but not before dropping another pile of reports on my desk to sign off on and to ask if I was okay.

"I'll be fine," I assured her. She smiled as she left and had her headphones in before the door was closed behind her.

When I heard the vacuums of the cleaning staff, I knew it was time to call it a day. I collected my briefcase and slowly made my way through the empty offices, took the elevator down to the basement, and walked like a zombie to my car.

I drove home in a daze with the words *midlife crisis* twirling through my mind. *Is that what this is? Is that what happened to Graham?* Did he wake up in a panic, realising that there wasn't some magic cut-off date that you passed to make you old, like you're young one day, pass some critical calendar date, then wake up old? It was simply something life ran towards at light speed, one day at a time. Had he panicked because he thought life was moving ahead without him?

I'd never thought about it before last Wednesday when Graham had dropped the bombshell that turned my life upside down. But maybe at thirty-five, my life was half over. I mean, Jesus. A lot of people died at seventy, and other people would just nod sadly and say they'd had a good life. But fuck, if my life was half over, I wasn't ready.

I had to make the most of what time I had left. And the truth was, if I didn't change my lifestyle choices now, maybe I wouldn't even get another thirty-five years. Or, at the very least, I wouldn't get a healthy thirty-five years.

So with that in mind, I went home and searched up more recipes. Like Reed had said, given cooking was my thing, I was going to make the best healthy food I possibly could. I took the healthy eating plan he had given me and made some adjustments. I'd let him look it over to approve, but if this was a long-term thing, I had to make it so it suited me.

And food really *was* my thing.

So I grilled myself some fish, added a fresh mango salsa served with a mixed green salad, and set the table to eat. But my motivated mood was short-lived when I saw that a table set for one was pretty fucking sad. And suddenly the apartment was too quiet, and I was again reminded that I was very much alone.

THE NEXT MORNING I was just as sore, if not a little sorer than the day before. But I was determined, and like a sucker for punishment, I dragged my sorry arse to the gym. I arrived with two minutes to spare, and Reed's whole face broke out into a smile when he saw me.

"Glad you made it."

"I'm sore as hell. Please make it stop."

"Okay," he said with a chuckle. "Come this way."

I followed him over to the far corner where there were mats on the floor. He said goodbyes to the people who were just finishing up and leaving, sweaty and smiling. It was pretty clear everyone liked him. He was just that type of guy. Not like me, I was socially awkward, said things that were cringeworthy at best. Like now...

"G'day," one fit looking guy said to me as he walked past.

"Good, thanks."

It wasn't until he was a metre or two behind me that I'd realised what I'd said. I just shook my head, like the socially inept idiot I was, and kept walking.

When we'd reached the corner, Reed stopped and turned to face me. "So, where does it hurt the most?"

"Everywhere."

"Legs? Arms? Chest?"

"Yes."

Reed smiled. "Okay then, sit down for me."

"Sitting down is fine. It's the getting up that bites."

Reed planted himself easily, gracefully, despite his size, on the ground. "Legs spread comfortably."

I lowered myself to the floor, trying to keep the grimace and yelp to a minimum. "Jesus. And this is normal?"

Reed nodded. "Take a deep breath, keep your chest up straight."

I did that and didn't die, so I relaxed a little.

"Now stretch forward and grab your ankles." He folded himself in half and held his feet with no trouble. I could barely reach past my knees. "Knees are fine."

"Ow."

He nodded encouragingly. "Hold it for twenty seconds."

Ugh. "I'm so unfit."

"But you're here."

I nodded and breathed through the stretch and burn in my hamstrings, but by the end of the twenty seconds, I was grabbing my calf muscles. At this point, I'd take any advance I could get. Then he had me stretch arms and shoulders, then my lower back. It probably took fifteen minutes, and I felt like I'd already done a workout session.

He leapt to his feet with the agility of a cat, then extended his hand to me. His hand was warm and calloused, which I had to admit, felt nice. I wasn't used to rough hands. Graham's hands were soft, like mine...

"So, we'll start on the treadmill to get the blood pumping." He obviously read the trepidation on my face. "Just slow, nothing strenuous."

I took a deep breath and stepped onto the machine. Once I started walking, Reed seemed to sigh in relief. "Perfect," he said.

He left me to it for a few minutes, and truthfully, it wasn't that hard. It was just hard on already-sore muscles. When that was done, I did equal time on the elliptical StairMaster, cardio-killing machine. It wasn't overly strenuous, but I could feel every muscle burn. After quite possibly the longest five minutes of my life, I stepped back off the machine, wiped my face down with my towel, and took a sip of water, trying not to die.

"How you feeling?" Reed asked.

"Like I've been set on fire, thanks for asking."

He just grinned and clapped his hands together enthusiastically. "Time for strength and core conditioning."

"I'm sorry, was that full strength coffee and air conditioning?"

He laughed, and his eyes shone bright blue. "Oh, you crack me up." Then he led me over to the weights. "The weight and pulley machine is good, but it might not always be available," he said. "Some days you might need to use free weights." He handed me two five kilo dumbbells, he picked up some for himself, and together we did a range of exercises like tricep extensions, lateral raises, and hammer curls. He called it body strength exercises. I called it brutality.

He put his weights down. "Okay, now get down on the floor for me."

I collapsed in a panting, sweating, aching heap. "Thank God."

Then he made me do cruel, cruel things like leg lifts, leg holds, bridges, and planking. And to finish, we did torso twists and sit ups. I mean I only did about thirty seconds of each, but good fucking Lord! And I signed up for this shit?

After he'd made sure I'd stretched properly and that I could still breathe and wasn't going to drop dead, he held his hand out to me where I was now lying flat on my back for a high-five. It was an effort to even lift my hand up to reach his, but I did it.

"Would you mind terribly if I just died here for a little while?"

He grinned. "Nope, no dying today." He held his hand to me and pulled me to my feet without any effort. "You did great."

"Can we go back to blinking? My eyelids are about the only things that still work."

He blinked once for yes.

I laughed and let my head fall forward, a mix of exhaustion and relief that my second official training session was finished.

"You did real good today, Henry." He spoke to me——and to all his clients, I presumed——like I was the only person in the room. "For the next two days, do some gentle walking, gentle stretches. Give your body a rest, but try not to be still for too long. And I'll see you on Sunday at eight o'clock, yeah?"

I nodded. "Yep. If I'm not dead."

"I'll text you tomorrow to see how you're getting on. Is that okay?"

"Sure. But isn't tomorrow your day off?"

Reed nodded. "Yep. I have Wednesdays and Fridays off. But I don't mind." He perked up and gave a mock salute. "It's my duty as your personal trainer."

I found myself smiling at him. "Sure. I better get going. I gotta go home and get showered and into work by nine."

"We have showers here."

I blanched. Never in a million years would I shower where anyone could walk in and see me. "Uh, no thanks."

Thankfully Reed didn't push it. Maybe he saw the fear on my face. He looked at his watch. "Shoot. It's eight o'clock now."

"Ten minutes to home, twenty minutes to shower and shave, and fifteen minutes to drive to work. Believe me, the longest part will be the walk from the elevator to my desk." I did my best rusted Tin Man impersonation, though I wasn't acting, and walked/shuffled out of the gym.

And by the time I fell into my office chair, the familiar yet still-surprising-at-every-turn muscle pain mowed me down again.

———

FRIDAY NIGHT I did nothing but eat grilled chicken and salad, wishing it was pizza, wishing I didn't hurt like hell, and wishing Graham hadn't left me. Saturday morning, even though I could barely move, I pottered around the apartment gathering up the bits of pieces of what remained of Graham's belongings. Well, anything below the knees could bloody well stay where it was because I couldn't bend down that far to pick it up.

By eleven o'clock, the dining table had a neat little collection of his things: his favourite coffee mugs, a red glazed bowl he bought from the Queen Victoria Markets from one of our many trips to Melbourne, a stack of DVDs which he clearly forgot to take with him, a pile of neatly folded clothes——most of which I had bought for him——some old books, an umbrella, some shoes, and a bunch of stuff from the bathroom vanity.

When he'd moved into my apartment, he hadn't brought that much stuff with him. No furniture, just mostly clothes and personal belongings, a box of kitchen utensils, and odd plates and cups. He left all his old mismatched furniture for his old flatmate when he'd moved out, considering I had everything we'd need.

But eight years later, there were now very visible gaps around my apartment of where his stuff used to be. The curved designer chaise he'd paid a small fortune for, the floor lamp which I always thought looked like a giant butt plug, the canvas off the wall in the hall, the centrepiece vase from the dining table...

There were also very visible gaps in my life. Eight years is a long time to spend with one person. We mostly had different social circles but there were some mutual friends, and I wondered idly who'd get whom in the split. I'd spoken with most of our closest friends during the week. Some were shocked at the news we'd broken up, some didn't seem too surprised at all. Like Colin and James, from their reaction, I gathered they knew it might have been coming for some time. Graham must have told them long before he told me, and I figured they'd be on the Graham side of the divide when the dust settled. And that was okay. Sure, they were great guys, but they'd always been closer to Graham.

With that in mind, I fished out my phone from my pocket, scrolled through recent calls, and hit Anika's name. She answered on the second ring. "Hey you."

"Hey."

"How are you today?"

"I'm going through the things Graham left behind."

"Oh. Did you need me to come around?"

"No, I'm okay."

"Gonna sell them on eBay? Or perform a ceremonial burning?"

"Well no, I was going to call him."

"Oh, Henry," she said quietly. "Don't do that to yourself. Burning everything will be much more therapeutic. I can bring around some petrol if you like."

"I'm not going to burn them."

"Then just text him."

"Why can't I call him? We were together for eight years. Surely I can call him?"

"What if he doesn't answer?" she asked gently. Then after a short silence, she added, "And what if he does?"

I sighed and plonked myself onto my couch. "Ow. Shit, goddammit. I keep forgetting I hurt all over."

"I applaud your efforts for getting healthy," Anika said. "But jeez, it sure sounds painful."

"It is."

"You sound miserable. Let me take you out for lunch."

I might have wallowed in my own pain and misery for a moment. "Will it involve pasta?"

"Do you want it to involve pasta?"

"Does a one legged duck swim in a circle?"

"A simple fuck yes would have sufficed."

"Then fuck yes."

"Okay, we'll pick you up in twenty minutes."

"God bless your soul."

She laughed and disconnected the call. Twenty minutes later, I was standing out the front of my apartment, trying to ease myself into the backseat of Anika's car. Sean, Anika's boyfriend, turned in his seat. "You okay?"

"Nope. I'm pretty sure I'm dying of some horrible disease that I Googled, but my personal trainer called it something more reasonable like sore muscles."

Sean made a face that was half amused, half sympathetic. "Ouch."

I liked Sean. He and Anika started dating a few years back, and he just slotted into our lives. He knew Anika and I were a package deal, there was rarely a day that went past that we didn't speak, and Sean had no issue with that.

After Graham had dumped me, I called Anika and she and Sean came straight over. It was Sean who bought the wine for us, and the food, and he gave me a big hug and listened, right along with Anika, as I sat on the floor and sobbed my stupid heart out. Now ten days later, he didn't look at me with the pity I would have expected. He just smiled warmly at me. "I hear pasta is on the agenda for today." Then he looked at Anika. "I've heard good things about a new place on Norton Street. Wanna check it out?"

Norton Street was synonymous with Italian food. It wasn't called *Little Italy* for no reason. "Sounds perfect," I said, even though he hadn't technically asked me. Anika was already heading toward Leichhardt.

It was perfect and just what I needed. It felt good to talk about other things, and the change of scene and being sociable were already making me feel half human again. I even ordered the tomato-based sauce with vegetables instead of the creamy bacon sauce I usually chose, and I even turned down the garlic bread.

Anika and Sean both stared at me like I'd been possessed by some freakish dieting alien. "What?" I retorted. "Do you know how long you have to run on a treadmill to burn just twenty calories?"

"Oh Jesus Christ, Henry, you're not gonna become one of *those* people are you?" Anika asked.

"What people?"

"The type of annoying healthy person that lectures on everything. Like a reformed smoker. You know the type: smoked like a chimney for years, they quit smoking then they change into some preacher of how disgusting it is."

"I won't change that much," I replied. "Because believe me, when this pasta comes out, I'm gonna suck those carbs down like a blowjob."

Sean choked on his drink, and Anika raised her glass to mine. "That's my boy."

WE TALKED about Anika's work, Sean's family and how much they adored Anika. Then we talked about my sister, my new exercise program, and of course, my new personal trainer.

I should have known Anika would latch on to that topic. "What kind of surname is Henske?"

I was confused. "The six letter kind?"

She rolled her eyes. "Is it German?"

"How the hell would I know?"

"Does he have an accent?"

"No."

"Is he gay?"

"I don't know."

"How can you not know?"

"Because I didn't ask him." I deliberately didn't mention the eggplant and lube conversation I'd had with him.

"Maybe you should."

"I'm not interested," I said. "Actually, I'm the complete opposite of interested. If there was an island of the fundamentally not interested, I'd be on it."

She ignored me. "Is he cute?"

I sighed. "Yes. He's built like a fridge, has a Colgate smile, and looks like one of those guys off a sports clothing ad."

"So, he's gorgeous?"

"I don't know. I'm still on the island of fundamentally not interested, where I will be forever."

She was suddenly serious. "No you won't. Maybe right now, but not forever." Anika's gaze softened. "Did you text Graham?"

"No. I still don't understand why you think I can't call him."

"Because you need to not hear his voice right now," Anika said. "And you definitely need to not see him."

"Why?"

Sean answered. "Because she doesn't want you to be hurt all over again. And she's right. You need space right now."

"I need him," I whispered.

"No you don't," they said in unison.

Anika smiled then added, "It's been ten days, and whether you know it or not, you've already started to move on."

"No I haven't."

"Yes you have. You've joined a gym, changed some eating habits. You're changing your life."

"For him," I added lamely. "I'm doing it for Graham."

Anika shook her head slowly. "You're doing it for you. Because you don't want to be the person you saw in the mirror ten days ago."

I had no answer for that.

Sean said, "And for what it's worth, fuck him."

Anika and I both stared at him.

"Sorry," he said with a not-sorry shrug. "But what Anika told you the day he left is right. If he doesn't love you at your worst, then he doesn't deserve to love you at your best."

Anika looked at Sean and melted. She kissed him on the cheek. "Awww, that's so sweet."

I gave him a smile. "Maybe. But if he called me right now and apologised and said he wanted to come back, I'd say yes."

"And that's why you shouldn't talk to him right now." Anika held out her hand. "Can I have your phone?"

I looked at her dubiously. "Why?"

"I'll text him on your behalf."

"I'm pretty sure I can do it."

"I know you, Henry. You'll stare at your phone for two hours, write out a hundred texts, and delete them all. You'll overthink it and you'll end up keeping his stuff and making a shrine out of it. We'll come to visit and you'll have a prayer corner devoted to him."

"Remember the time with *Sex and the City*?" Sean added softly. "With the whole shrine to Samantha Jones?"

"That doesn't count. I was sick with fever and possibly delusional. And Samantha Jones is like my idol, so shut up."

Anika raised her eyebrow at me and stuck her hand in my face, palm up. "Phone, Henry."

I handed it over, and watched her as she said out loud

what she was typing. "Hi, you left some things at my place, like your balls and your backbone, you gutless fuck."

"Anika!"

She showed me the screen and had, thankfully, not typed in the last part. "Let me know by Friday if you want to collect them. Thanks."

"Why Friday?" I asked.

"You're giving him a deadline," she explained. "It tells him, one, you're not waiting forever, and, two, no explanation of what happens to said belongings if he doesn't collect them. That tells him you hold no sentimental attachment, because fuck him."

"Oh."

She gave me a bright smile. "Then by this time next week, if he still hasn't collected them, I'll bring around the petrol for that ceremonial burning I was looking forward to." Then she made a thoughtful, somewhat sad face. "We might give him two weeks. That way, with a bit of luck, if or when he does call around, you'll have realised you're better off without him."

I sighed. "I'm trying to remember why I ever thought your blunt-force honesty was an endearing quality."

"Two weeks is for your benefit, not his," she said, typing away on my phone. She held it out and showed me. It was a short and direct request to come and collect his things, asking him to reply to the text first. I assumed that was so I could let Anika know when he was coming around so she could be at my place when he turned up. "Happy for me to send him the text?"

I thought about it for a moment and nodded, and before I could change my mind, she pressed Send. She slid my phone across the table to me and the wait staff cleared our plates, and not a moment later, my phone beeped with a message.

I startled and went to grab the phone, but the sudden movement jarred the sore muscles in my arm. "Ow."

Anika snatched up the phone and read the screen.

"Is it him?" I asked, unable to hide the hope in my voice.

She shook her head. "Reed Henske," she replied. "Wants to know how you're feeling today?"

"Oh." I couldn't help but smile and held out my hand for my phone. "Can I have my phone?"

Anika shook her head. "No, I got this one too."

"Anika, please don't."

But she was already typing. *Hi Reed. This is Anika, Henry's best friend.*

She hit Send and gave me that daring smirk that made me and Sean both sigh. My phone beeped almost immediately. Anika read his reply out loud. "Is Henry okay?" She made a sappy face. "Awww, he's sweet!" Then she replied to his text, *He's fine. Whinging that he's sore every time he moves, but fine.*

Then a complete text conversation happened between them without me.

That's good. Will he be in tomorrow for his session?

Yes, he'll be there.

Good.

Can I ask you something?

Sure.

Henske. Is it German?

Yes.

How old are you?

31.

"Thirty-one?" I mumbled. "God, he looks twenty-two."

Henry just said, "Shit you don't look that old." LOL These are all the questions Henry was too scared to ask you, by the way.

That's fine. Can I ask you something?

Anika did a little dance in her seat and quickly typed out her reply. *Yes.*

"No," I interrupted. "Can I have my phone back please?"

Anika grinned. "Nope."

Then my phone beeped again with Reed's next message. *Is Henry always so funny?*

Anika quickly replied, *Always. Except for now. He's pissed I won't give him his phone back.* Then she snapped a photo of me and sent it before I could stop her.

She slid my phone back to me with a laugh. Then, in a sing-song voice, she said, "He thinks you're funny."

"Still on that island of not interested," I said, now frowning at the horrible photo of me she sent him. "You can pay for lunch," I told her then quickly typed out a response to Reed, speaking the words out loud as I typed. "This is Henry. Apologies for Anika's questions. Just so you know, she's been demoted to worst best friend ever." I gave Anika a snarly glare. "Yes, I'll be there tomorrow at eight."

His reply was almost immediate. *Are you eating at Tre Vini? The background of your photo looks familiar. I love that place.*

I texted straight back. *Yes! First time here. Great food. I wanted pasta. But just so you know, I had the healthiest thing on the menu.*

Good man! Enjoy your carbo-coma. See you tomorrow.

"Henry, you're smiling at your phone," Anika said. I looked up to find them both staring at me.

"What? Don't look at me like that. I told you before, I am one hundred percent not interested. He's a nice guy. He understands what I'm putting my body through, and so what if he texts me to see how I'm doing. Isn't that what all personal trainers do?"

Anika and Sean shook their heads slowly. "Not really," Sean added. "Unless he's a life coach or well-being mentor or whatever they're calling themselves these days. Is that what you signed up for?"

"Well, no." I hesitated. "He's just my personal trainer."

"Who has your number and texts you," Anika prodded.

"Yes. To see how I'm holding up, that's all. I thought it was nice."

Sean grinned. "Next thing you know he'll be accidentally running into you in the supermarket."

Oh God.

"Oh my God," Anika said, a slow grin spreading across her face. "He has already? Jeez, he's moving fast!"

"What? No! It wasn't like that," I protested quickly. "He lives close by, apparently. It's our mutual supermarket. People are allowed to have a mutual supermarket. He suggested I go shopping for my new diet plan before I went home because he knew I wouldn't be able to get up once I sat down."

Anika side-eyed me. "So, he knew you were going to be there? And just so happened to turn up as well? Interesting."

I shook my head. "It's not interesting. It was just a coincidence." Anika pursed her lips together, and before she could say one more thing about it, I added, "Please don't go there. I'm so not ready for that. My heart is broken, and I can't see myself ever being ready for that. I mean, Graham might not love me anymore, but I can't just turn my heart off." I swallowed hard. "And anyway, if you saw Reed, you'd understand why you're being completely absurd. He's... well, I'm hardly his type. I don't even know if he's... inclined to be interested. Not that it matters, because I'm on the island of indefinitely not interested."

Anika's face softened. "Oh, Henry, I'm sorry. I didn't mean to push. Of course it's too soon."

Sean turned the empty glass in his hand. "Don't sell yourself short, Henry. Graham was a dickhead for leaving, and it's his loss. And it will be some lucky bloke's gain, just you wait and see."

Anika stared at Sean, as did I. It was the most heartfelt thing I'd heard him say. "Awww," Anika cooed. She nudged his shoulder with hers. "You're so getting lucky tonight."

He turned a deep-pink shade of embarrassed, and while they were looking all lovey-dovey into each other's eyes, I stood up, only merely wincing in pain. "Being nice to me and sickly in love doesn't count. You're still paying."

They laughed as they followed me to the maître d's table where Anika cheerfully handed over her credit card. The drive home was kinda quiet, though I felt a lot better than I had this morning. When Anika pulled up out the front of my place, she turned in her seat. "I'll call you tonight, okay?" She waited for me to nod. "And if Graham replies to that text, call me before you do anything, okay?"

Oh. I'd already forgotten about that text... "Sure."

With my better mood suddenly deflated, I faced my dining table full of Graham's belongings, and I felt more than deflated. I was back to square one.

And although I'd hoped, and although I checked my phone a dozen times, he never replied.

FIVE

My sullen mood followed me into the gym on Sunday morning. Reed was his usual bright and cheery self, grinning when he saw me. "Hey!"

"Hey," I replied back.

He clearly picked up on my lack of lustre, and his brow furrowed for a second. His smile slid away. "Everything okay?"

"Yeah, yeah," I said, trying to smile. "Just feeling sorry for myself. Ignore me."

He seemed a little unsure of what to say next, and I hated that I'd made him uncomfortable. "You sure?"

"Yep. What torture are you going to put me through today?"

"That depends. How are you feeling? Still sore?"

"I'm actually not too bad. I'm either getting better, or I'm just used to the pain." To be honest, I did still hurt, but with my broken heart giving one last hurrah, it kind of paled in comparison.

I'm certain Reed saw right through me because he didn't push me too hard. He had me do the usual treadmill and elliptical hell, then we did weights on the cable and pulley machine. If Reed wasn't with me, standing beside me, he was watching me.

I knew I was pushing myself. But the harder I pushed, the better I felt. I could feel the stress leaving my mind, and the more I worked my muscles and made my lungs burn, the better I felt.

"Okay, that'll do," Reed said, effectively putting a stop to my low-pulley raises. "Or you *will* be sore tomorrow."

I took a second to catch my breath, and he reset the machine. He handed me my towel. "Wanna talk about it?"

I wiped my face down and shook my head. "Voldemort."

"Ah." Reed nodded knowingly. "Thought it might be."

"You'd think after eight years together I might deserve a reply to a text message, but apparently not."

"Oh." He chewed on his bottom lip for a moment. "Yes. You do deserve a reply text."

"Sorry, I wasn't going to talk about it," I mumbled. "But I only texted him to tell him he can come and pick his shit up. I don't want it in my house anymore. But no, not even a one-word reply. Maybe Anika was right. Maybe I should torch the lot of it. Actually, if I haven't heard from him by next Friday, that's exactly what I'll do."

"You'll set it on fire?"

"Yep. Not inside the house, of course, but a ceremonial burning outside."

Reed nodded thoughtfully. "Of course."

I let out a sigh. "I guess I'm at the anger stage of the process. Denial didn't last as long as I thought it would."

He gave me a sad smile. "I'm sorry you're going through this."

"I'm sorry my friend Anika sent you a bunch of inappropriate questions. And they weren't things I wanted to know, per se, just questions I didn't have answers to when she asked."

He was smiling genuinely now and went through the

usual stretches with me. When we were quiet for a moment, he said, "Anika seems great."

"She is."

"Okay, pull your arm across your chest for me; feel it stretch the shoulder." I did as he said, then he asked. "What's the Anika story?"

Why did he want to know about Anika…? Oh. *Oh*. I had to admit, after Anika and Sean ribbing me yesterday about Reed being interested in me——even though I wasn't ready for that——had been flattering, and the confirmation that he wasn't interested in me at all was a little disappointing. "She's been my best friend since college. We studied microeconomics together and just clicked. Though we tend to act like twelve year olds when we get together. She's actually the head of her accounts department for Myer. Stylish, gorgeous. But she's taken, sorry. Her boyfriend, Sean, is a great guy."

Confusion flashed across his face before realisation kicked in. "Oh! Oh no," he said with an embarrassed laugh. "No, I'm not interested. But thanks."

Okay then. Hardly surprising, though. "I didn't think you'd be single," I admitted. "Guy like you…"

He let his arms fall down to his sides. "A guy like me?"

Shit, was he offended? "Oh, I just mean you're hot, got a great body, fit as hell, super nice, you know. A guy like you."

He laughed, more to himself than at me, and his ears tinged pink. "Um, thanks? But no, I'm single. I was seeing someone…"

"But now you're not," I finished for him. "So you know what breakups are like?"

He nodded slowly. "Oh yeah."

I wasn't going to ask, but then I thought, what the hell? "Was it your choice?"

"Yep. Didn't make it any easier, though."

I frowned at that. "I'm pretty sure it's harder being the one that gets told you're past your use-by date."

"I'm pretty sure finding your boyfriend getting a blowjob from a stranger in a bathroom is worse."

I stared at him. Then I stared some more. Well, shit. *Boyfriend?* Well, I'll be damned. He was right, though. At least Graham didn't cheat on me. "Yep, you win."

Reed let out a heavy sigh. "Sorry. I shouldn't have said that. That was out of line."

"No it wasn't. It was perfectly fine. Apart from your ex being a cheating piece of shit. That's not fine at all."

Now he laughed. "It was six months ago. I'm over it. But yes, you're right. He was a cheating piece of shit."

"And a complete idiot to ruin a relationship with you," I added.

His smile turned kinda shy. "Thanks."

I stopped stretching my shoulder and shook out my arm. "I think I might've overdone it today. Just imagine how buff I'll be if this anger phase lasts for a while."

Reed laughed at that. "I bet you feel better though."

I took a second to assess myself. Sure, my body hurt, but my mind was surprisingly clear. "I do."

Reed clapped my shoulder. "Good."

I gathered my water bottle and gym bag and groaned when I stood upright. "My plan for the rest of the day is to do some menu planning for the week, maybe some groceries, then to plant my arse in front of the television and catch up on *Game of Thrones.*"

Reed sighed. "Sounds perfect. I'm doing much the same. Though there's a farmers market in the park at Drummoyne today. I was gonna head over and see what's on offer."

"Oh, I've seen that sometimes when I've driven past but never called in."

"First Sunday of every month," Reed said. "They have some great stuff. Fresh, locally grown, some organic. They have some gourmet sauces you might like. All homemade."

"Sounds good," I agreed. "I was going to try a new salmon recipe. And I found a grilled pork fillet with apple and chili recipe. It looked good too."

He brightened. "Oh my God, I made this calamari with lime and chili the other night. It was so good."

"You'll have to give me the recipe. I love trying new things."

"Me too! I'll bring it in for you. Or I can text it to you."

"Sounds good." Then I thought of something. I'd only seen him walking or riding a pushbike, which I didn't see out the front today, which meant he must've walked to work. "Will you walk or ride your bike to the market?"

"Yeah, I'll ride. It's not far. I wear a backpack to carry stuff, so it's no big deal."

"Did you want a lift? What time do you finish up here?"

"Oh, not for another hour." He hesitated. "It's fine, thanks anyway."

"By the time I get home and showered, grab my menu planner, it'll be an hour. Believe me, my arms will be so sore it'll take me twenty minutes to put socks on. And I literally drive past the gym on my way."

He fought a smile. "Are you sure?"

"Absolutely."

"Then that'd be great."

"Okay, I'll be back in an hour. I'll just wait out front."

His smile was warm and wide. "Sure thing."

An hour later, at ten o'clock exactly, I pulled back into the gym car park, and whether or not he was watching for me, I had no clue, but Reed walked out with a gym bag in his hand. He smiled as he opened the door and got into the front seat. He slid in easily, despite his size, and again I was reminded of his fridge-like frame as he filled his half of the front of my sports car.

"Thanks again for doing this," he said, stuffing his bag under his feet. "And when we get to the markets, we might wanna put my gym bag in the boot. I mean, there's nothing disgusting in there, but no gym bag smells great."

I pulled the car back onto the road into the always-steady stream of traffic. "No problem. Actually, thank you for reminding me about the markets. I've always been meaning to go but just never got there."

"They're really good. Well, I think so," he amended. "I love fresh produce and getting inspired to try new things."

"Me too!" I said. I stopped at a red light and grabbed my menu planner from the centre console and handed it to him. "Here, have a look through that. There's an app on my phone for it as well, so I can download new recipes and whatnot. I just printed this week's plan to bring with me."

"Oh, this looks good," he said, nodding to the first page. "You could do this one vegetarian as well."

I squinted at him. "Well, I could."

Reed laughed. "Like your meat, I take it."

"I'm gay, so yes. In all forms." The tips of his ears turned pink as he smiled, so I apologised. "Sorry. No filter, remember."

"It's all good. Don't apologise." He looked out over the water as we crossed the Iron Cove Bridge. "Your friends and family must be used to you and your lack of filter."

"Uh, yes."

"And the people you work with?"

"Actually, no. Only my personal assistant, Melinda, is. She's used to me. But no one else." I sighed. "I don't talk to anyone else, really."

"At all?"

"Not if I can avoid it."

"You choose not to talk to them?" Reed frowned. "Is that a management thing? Because you don't seem the type to snob your co-workers based on pay rate."

That made me snort. "Oh God no! It's not a pay rate thing. It's a 'me being a filterless idiot' thing." I pulled into a parking spot at the markets and turned off the engine. "When I first started there, Gr——" I stopped short of saying his name. "I mean Voldemort suggested I not talk to people up front. You know, wait until they got to know me and liked me before they heard some of the things that come out of my mouth."

A little line appeared between his eyebrows. "He suggested you don't talk to people?"

I nodded. "Not exactly nice of him, but I could see his point. I mean, in staff meetings I would say nothing instead of calling the national marketing manager a fucking idiot. So it kind of worked. In six years I've had two promotions for simply putting my head down and getting my work done. There's a lot to be said about being the overweight unattractive guy. Kind of invisible, or more to the point, no one sees me as a threat, so I kinda sneak through, ya know? But now people are used to me not saying much, just keeping to myself, and it's too late to change."

Reed was quiet for a long moment, and I wondered which part of what I'd just said he didn't agree with the most. "I don't know much about the corporate world. I'll be the first to admit that. And maybe what Voldemort said was plausible, but," he shook his head, "I dunno. I'd just never tell anyone to not be who they are. And who knows, maybe the national marketing manager was a fucking idiot——"

"With terrible fashion sense."

He smiled. "With terrible fashion sense. Who knows? Maybe that needed saying."

I chuckled at that. "Or not. I love my job, and being in the corporate world comes with certain stipulations that I dress and behave a certain way. It's not all bad. I'm quieter at work, but I'd imagine the majority of people in corporate finance don't fly their freak flag at their place of employment." I nodded to the park up ahead, to the crowds looking at stalls as they strolled through the market. "Shall we get out?"

Reed climbed out of my car, and it wasn't until I had to stand up that I was rudely reminded of the muscle pain in my legs. And back. And arms and shoulders and holy shit. "Ow. Okay, I think I overdid it."

Reed gave me a sympathetic smile. "You poor thing."

I straightened up and rolled my shoulders. Well, tried to. "Why did you let me push myself so hard today?"

He laughed at that. "Uh, because you were pissed off at Voldemort, remember?"

"Oh yeah." I sighed as I hobbled toward him. "I forgot."

He looked me up and down. "You'll be okay?"

"Just out of interest, how many calories does dropping dead burn?"

Reed snorted. "You're not going to drop dead, Henry."

And suddenly I caught a whiff of something and I perked right up, my sore and aching muscles momentarily forgotten. "Can I smell coffee?"

Reed laughed and answered his own question. "Yeah, you'll be fine."

I made a beeline for the coffee van. "Do you drink coffee?" I asked Reed.

"Yeah, sure." He fished out his wallet from his pants.

"No, let me get this, please," I said, offering to pay. "Unless you drink decaf on soy or something else as equally horrifying."

Reed chuckled. "Nope, no decaf for me. Never did see the point."

"Exactly!" I looked up at the guy in the coffee van and told him my order and waited for Reed to do the same. I handed over some cash, and when we were given our coffees, Reed looked truly grateful.

"Thank you," he said quietly.

I smiled at his sincerity. "You're welcome."

"Okay," he said, looking around the market stalls. "What's first on your list?"

So we spent a while strolling the market and searching out the ingredients on my menu plan. Reed found some lemon butter he'd run out of, and he insisted I buy some too. Then he wanted me to try a fig and chili chutney. "You have to try it," he said. "I have it at home. It's great on grilled chicken with salad."

The little old lady selling the homemade jars of goods grinned at him. "You bought some last time," she said, her Greek accent strong. She obviously remembered him. I figured it was hard not to remember the six foot three inches tall, fridge sized, clean-cut gorgeous man. "You try it on lamb too," she said. "I also spread thin on filo pastry, fine chop nuts and bake. Sprinkle with icing sugar. Make my husband very happy."

"Okay, sold," I said, happily handing over my money. I couldn't believe how nice everyone was and how fresh all the produce was. I also couldn't believe I'd lived just across the river for years and had never been to these markets. The sun was shining, people were walking dogs, jogging around the edge of the river, everyone was talking or laughing, and the coffee was great. "Thank you," I said to Reed. "For suggesting to come here. It's amazing."

His smile was huge. "It's great, isn't it?"

"Oh look!" I said as we moved to another stall. This one sold home-baked gourmet dog treats, which I wasn't too interested in, but they also had some boxes of second-hand books. I couldn't resist having a peek, and I smiled victoriously as I pulled out a ratty old copy of *Harry Potter and the Philosopher's Stone*. "I'm buying this for you," I told Reed.

He made a face. "Really?"

"Yes really. You can't be the only person on the planet not to have read these books."

"Aren't they for kids?"

I gasped and put the book to my chest. "Oh, *silencio*."

"What?"

"Never mind." I paid the bank-breaking price of a dollar for the well-read, well-used book, and slid it into one of his bags. "You're welcome."

He laughed. "I'm not ungrateful. I'm just not convinced it's my thing."

"Read it. And if you don't like it, then you don't have to read the other six."

He snorted. "Deal."

I found myself grinning at him. "Did you get everything you need?" He had a range of veggies and eggs, some handmade Italian pasta, and a jar of the lemon butter.

"Oh yeah, this is everything. And even better that I don't have to cram it into my backpack to ride home."

"You don't drive at all?" I asked as we walked back to my car, carrying our bags of goods.

"Nope. I ride or walk to work because I live so close, and if I need to head out of Balmain, I catch a bus or take the ferry."

"Have you lived in Balmain long?"

"Nah, only six months."

Ah, six months. About the time he split with his cheating ex. "So, you moved here after you broke up with your boyfriend?" Then I realised that question was way too personal. "Sorry, you don't have to answer that. I didn't mean to cross a line."

"No, it's fine. Like I said, I'm over it. I can talk about it." He stopped at my car and waited for me to unlock it. "His name was Brett, and we'd been seeing each other for about a year. We didn't live together or anything, but we were exclusive. Well, we were supposed to be. When it all happened, I needed a change of scene, so I moved closer to work. Best thing I ever did. I love it here."

I pressed the button to unlock my car and popped the boot. "Where did you move from?"

Reed put his bags into the boot with mine, alongside his gym bag. "I used to live in Five Dock. My lease was up around the same time, and I thought the move would do me good."

"Fair enough."

"You rent or own your place?" he asked as we climbed into my car.

"I own it. I was given a helping hand by my grandmother's estate, but my mortgage is still enough to cause heart palpitations."

He seemed impressed. "I bet it is. But you're a professional when it comes to hypothetical risk management, right?"

That made me smile. I really liked that he understood what my job entailed. "Something like that."

I drove back to Balmain and asked for directions to his place. I pulled up out front of the apartment block, wondering how I could tell him I enjoyed the morning with him without making things awkward, but he spoke first. "Do you realise you walked around for the last hour or so and not once complained about being sore?"

"I'm still sore," I admitted. "I'm pretty sure I'll be impersonating a T-Rex by dinner time, but I think the distraction helped. I should thank you for this morning. I enjoyed it."

He smiled warmly. "Me too."

"I'm pretty sure I would've been sitting at home wallowing in self-pity and getting sorer the more I sat around and did nothing."

"The walking around really helps."

"And the coffee, and the sunshine, and the company," I added. "So thank you."

"Glad I could help take your mind off Voldemort not replying to your text."

Oh God. "I'd forgotten about that."

He looked stricken. "Shit. I'm sorry."

I barked out a laugh. "No, please don't apologise." Jeez, this morning was a good distraction. I hadn't thought about Graham in hours. "It was a great Voldemort-free morning. We should check out food markets more often."

His smile was back. "Any time."

I got out of my car and popped the boot, and Reed quickly gathered up his bags and his gym bag. "I'll let you know how that recipe goes."

"Yes. I'd like that."

"I'll see you Tuesday?"

"Yep, bright and early," he said, walking toward his apartment block. "Have a great date with Jon Snow."

"Who?"

"Jon Snow? You know, *Game of Thrones*?"

"Oh." God, I felt like an idiot. "I will. Though Renly Baratheon is probably more my type."

He laughed at that. "Bye Henry."

I waved him off and got back into my car. I smiled as I drove home, only feeling the pull of sore muscles every so often that afternoon. I cooked my grilled salmon and salad then sent Reed a photo of it with the TV in the background paused on a close up of Renly.

He replied a short while after with a photo of his dinner. It looked like grilled chicken with some kind of rice salad. But that wasn't what made me smile. Because of what I saw in the top of the photo, almost off screen and probably obscure to most people, but I recognised it for what it was. The Harry

Potter book was open, face down, like he'd had to stop reading it to take the photo.

Still smiling, I texted out a reply. *Dinner looks great. You'll have to send me the recipe. Glad to see Harry's keeping you company while you dine.*

His reply made me laugh out loud. *Oh, silencio.*

Six

THE NEXT TWO WEEKS PASSED IN A BLUR OF WORK meetings, reports, and deadlines. I was home later than normal and spent my nights trying new recipes and experimenting with healthier options that suited me. The crazy thing was, as busy as I was, my gym sessions kept me focused. I pushed myself hard, with Reed a constant by my side, and he was right: by the third week of my exercise program, I wasn't anywhere near as sore.

Sure, some things hurt. Like reaching right above my head to get folders from the top shelf at work or getting down on all fours to retrieve a pen that rolled under my sofa at home. But the normal, everyday stuff was fine.

And the even crazier thing was, I was actually starting to enjoy my workouts. It wasn't a case of making myself go, under sufferance, like I had no choice in the matter. I was looking forward to hitting the gym, and if I was completely honest, I looked forward to seeing Reed. His smile was always warm and wide whenever I walked through the door, and even though he probably treated all his clients with the same enthusiasm, it still felt good. He helped me with my techniques; he encouraged me to push myself a little harder. He had complete faith that I could achieve whatever goals he set for me.

And that kind of faith, that absolute reassurance, was everything I needed.

My Thursday morning session with him was just like normal. We did cardio, then core strength, then some weights for my legs and arms. And although it wasn't uncommon for him to leave me to it for a few minutes at a time, this time he didn't. He did the exercises with me, all the while talking about the recipes he'd made, when two guys walked past us over to the free weights. One of them in particular was all suggestive smiles and bedroom eyes at Reed and probably couldn't have tried much harder to get Reed's attention.

"I think someone's interested," I said quietly, nodding to where the guys were.

"Hm." Reed just kind of shrugged it off but turned and faced the opposite way from where they were setting up their weights. He spoke in a murmur that only I could hear. "He is. He asked me out."

"Oh." I tried to act all cool because this was apparently top secret. "When?"

"The other week. I told him I wasn't ready."

"And that's fair enough."

"Well, it's nicer than saying I wasn't interested." He took a sip of his water. "He's not my type."

I looked back at the guy in question and had to admit I wasn't surprised. I mean, he was buff but really over-muscled, and whereas Reed looked the picture of health and fitness, this guy could be the poster boy for "Why Not to do Steroids."

I shrugged one shoulder. "His muscles look so fake he could pass as a balloon animal."

Reed almost spat his water. He coughed and choked as he tried to cover his laughter.

"Please don't die of second degree drowning. Or bubble

boy might run over and give you CPR." I wiped my face down with my towel and felt kinda bad for taking the piss out of a guy I didn't even know. "I'm sure he's probably a very nice guy, and I of all people shouldn't be judging on appearances."

"It's not his appearance that doesn't interest me," he explained.

I figured as much. I mean, seriously, Reed was ripped as hell. Of course he'd find guys like that attractive. But not only just physical appearances. Reed would need someone who was like-minded in caring for their bodies and fitness, not an overweight guy like me who cries and wheezes his way through a five minute treadmill walk.

"I can see why," I said, aiming for nonchalant. "I mean, if balloon animals are your thing."

He chuckled. "No, it's not that. I can't even have a conversation with him. Every time he speaks to me, he asks me what protein powder I use or what weight I bench-pressed this week. Then tells me what he's done, whether I ask for it or not. Like it's a competition or something. I don't know. It's just awkward."

"Maybe he's shy and doesn't know what else to talk about with you," I offered. "Maybe he's so dazzled by your dashing good looks that he's rendered an idiot every time he talks to you."

Reed laughed at that and shook his head. "Not likely."

"And anyway, all we've ever really talked about is food," I countered. "Is that awkward?"

He balked. "No, no. Not at all. I love food. I love that we talk recipes and about non-work related things, and you taking me to the markets this last weekend was a highlight."

"Good," I said adamantly. "Because I made a citrus tart with that lemon butter. It was on some health food site I found, and I had to improvise, but it is so good. I'll have to send you the recipe."

"Oh, yes please. Sounds great! I never thought about using it like that. I found a site that has great ideas. I'll have to forward you the link."

Someone called Reed's name, and it was then I realised the time. "Holy shit. I'm gonna be late."

I waved my goodbyes and raced out the door and drove home like a maniac for the quickest shower of my life. Sure, I was running late for work, but I still had time to cut a slice of the tart and slip it into a container. I put the rest of the tart into another container to take to work because I certainly didn't want to eat it all. Then because I was already going to be five minutes late, I figured I may as well be ten minutes late. So I pulled up at the gym, dressed in my work suit, hair brushed and clean shaven, and dropped the container on the reception desk.

Reed was over at the rowing machines with another client, so I just smiled at him and called out, "For you," before I raced back outside.

I got to work, and thankfully no one but Melinda had realised I was late. "You're looking awfully happy this morning," she said cautiously.

Before she could ask for details or hypothesise on any reason her imagination could come up with, I handed her the rest of the citrus tart. "For morning tea." She took the container like it was a dose of herpes just as my phone beeped. It was two messages from Reed. First, a picture of the empty container I'd sent him, save a few crumbs in the bottom. And a text that followed.

Oh. My. God. I need the recipe for that.

I grinned at my phone, then at Melinda. "I am happy this morning," I said to her. I sat at my desk and opened emails first, then a job folder from my in tray. It wasn't until about thirty minutes later that I realised I was actually happy. For the first time in weeks, since Graham had popped my cosy bubble and I thought I'd never find a reason to smile again, I was doing okay.

I found the recipe online, sent a copy of it to Reed with a few notations of what I'd improvised on, and spent the rest of my day powering through my workload with an energy I hadn't felt in years.

I hadn't given my citrus tart another thought until I stopped for lunch and made my way into the lunchroom. I ordered a salad and sat at my usual table away from everyone else when someone——Lydia, I think her name was——stopped by my table. "That lemon tart was delicious, thank you!" she said before quickly making her way out the door.

Then someone else stopped and waited for me to look at them. A pretty girl with red hair who I'd seen before but had no clue of her name. "Did you make morning tea? Because it was divine. Thank you."

Then Kadin. And then Lena, and then Rihanti. I'd worked with these people for years and never said more than was professionally polite. They all wanted to tell me how much they loved my cooking and how they appreciated the gesture.

"Oh, you're welcome," I said awkwardly. I put my fork down. "I didn't want to eat it all myself, but I love to cook. And I went to a fresh produce market and got inspired, but I'm trying to lose weight, so I thought I'd bring it in here. I actually thought Melinda would just take it home. I didn't know she was going to serve it up to everyone."

God, this is why I didn't speak to people I worked with. I literally just sprayed them with verbal diarrhoea. They stared at me. "Oh." Rihanti spoke first. "I'm sorry, was she not supposed to share it?"

Great Henry, the first time they ever speak to you, and you make them feel bad. "Oh! No, I don't mind. I'm happy that she shared it, actually. And I'm really glad you liked it!"

They seemed to relax. Then Kadin said, "We should take it in turns to cook and bring something in. Like every Monday, someone brings something different in for morning tea. They do that at my father's work, and everyone loves it."

"Yes!" Lena chimed in. "We should! We should make sure no one has allergies or anything like that though."

"Oh crap." I must've said that out loud because the three of them looked at me. I cleared my throat. "I mean, jeez. That was something I didn't think about before Melinda offered my citrus tart. It'd be just my luck someone would die of anaphylactic shock because of me."

And there was my filterless brain again. They were back to staring at me, so I picked up my fork and stabbed a cherry tomato like it was its fault I was socially inept.

Then Rihanti laughed. "Or me. That type of thing usually happens to me."

Then Lena grabbed Rihanti's arm. "Oh my God. When I was in primary school, it was a cake day sale and I brought in some cupcakes my mum and I had made, and some little kid had an egg allergy. Wasn't pretty."

Then Kadin mentioned a time when he knew of some girl who served dog food on sandwiches to girls who were total bitches to her.

Rihanti, Lena, and I both stared at him. It was completely gross and completely not related to what we were talking about and very much how most of my conversations ended up. I realised that maybe Kadin and I had more in common than I first realised and made a mental note that I liked him now and would make an effort to be awkward with him together.

I couldn't help but laugh. "I hope she told them what they ate."

He just shrugged. "Nope. Just has the satisfaction in knowing, that's all."

"Anyway," Lena said with a smile, "thanks again for the lemon tart. And we'll put a memo out to see if anyone's interested in doing a Monday morning tea share thing. It was good to speak to you."

"Yes," Rihanti agreed. "And I can tell you've been dieting these last few weeks. You look great."

"Oh." I blinked a few times. Her compliment threw me for a six. It had been years since I'd received a compliment, and I wasn't sure what to say. "Um. Thanks?"

"You can tell," Kadin added. "That you're dieting."

Okay, so now I wanted to crawl under the table. Thankfully, like a come-save-your-boss alarm went off, Melinda came to my rescue. She sat down across from me, totally diverting their attention. "I'll send the lemon tart recipe out in a blind copy," she declared to no one in particular. "If I can get him to share it."

They all seemed pleased by this, and I breathed a sigh of relief when they left us to eat our lunch in peace. "You okay?" Melinda asked gently.

"Yes, I'm fine. They just made small talk, and apparently I've instigated a Monday morning tea cook off. Which I'm totally blaming on you because you served the lemon tart to them. And now it will surely be expected that I have regular conversations with co-workers. I already blabbered on like an idiot in front of them. Though I think Kadin and I might be able to contend for 'Australia's most awkward conversation' contest. He seems nice, though, despite the dog-food sandwich comment."

Melinda's only reaction to my entire tirade was a slight flicker of her eyebrow. "How's your lunch?"

I looked at my half-eaten salad. "Oh. It's good. How's yours?"

She bit into her chicken salad wrap and made a half-committed assent type noise. "Hmm."

"They said they could tell I'd been dieting."

Melinda swallowed her food. "You can. Your suit hides a lot, but you can tell around your face and neck."

"Oh."

"That was a compliment, Henry."

I grimaced. "I know. Compliments make me uncomfortable."

She smiled as she bit into her wrap. When she'd finished eating, she said, "Anika called. You're going out tomorrow night."

"Am I?"

"Have you ever won an argument with Anika?"

"Good point." I closed the lid on my empty salad container and set the fork on top of it. "What time and where?"

"Seven o'clock at The London."

The London was a popular hotel within stumbling distance to my place. Which is where we frequented when it was my turn to get shitfaced. "Did she elaborate on the occasion?"

"She said it would be Friday and you hadn't heard from Graham about his belongings."

My stomach turned and my heart squeezed. "Oh yeah. I forgot. Maybe he's busy."

Melinda made a thoughtful face like him being busy was a possibility. "Or, maybe he's a selfish arsehole who did you a favour by leaving."

I sighed. "I take it you and Anika had a little chat."

"Yes. She's bringing BBQ starters and lighter fluid to your place on Saturday morning for a ritual burning of what he left behind."

Me, I thought sourly. *He left me behind.*

"She also said you've been conversing with your personal trainer more than is required, and I might have mentioned your smile and mood this morning when you arrived."

I gasped. "Oh no you didn't."

"Yes, I did." Her poker face was frightening. "I said I hadn't seen you smile like that in a long time."

"There's nothing going on between Reed and me. I've told Anika this, and I even explained the island called I'm Not Ready For That, which I'm currently stranded on." I sniffed. "And just because Reed and I talk and text and spent a few hours at the food market together, doesn't mean anything. He's a nice guy, he's helping me achieve my goals, and he likes food. We have things in common. That's not a crime."

The corner of her eyebrow flicked again, but her lips remained pursed.

"And just because we're both gay and he's gorgeous and the size of a fridge, doesn't mean anything either. Two gay men can have a platonic relationship," I whispered across the table. "It's not all about sex. And anyway, he's so far out of my league, we're not even on the same planet."

She stared at me for a long uncomfortable second. "You finished convincing yourself yet?"

"Not even close. And you and Anika aren't allowed to talk to each other anymore. I prohibit it."

She rolled her eyes. "Really?"

"Yes."

Melinda let out a long-suffering sigh. "You have a two o'clock with Lillian, and I emailed you the Kerual account file."

I huffed, disappointed that she didn't bite at anything I just said. "Thank you."

"You're welcome."

Without another word, we both stood up and put our rubbish in the bin. I held the door open for her, and we walked in stubborn silence to my office door. I waited for a moment, wondering if I should say anything that wouldn't make my *convincing myself* any worse, but she spoke instead.

"Everyone who tried your lemon tart loved it, Henry. It was the perfect excuse for you to talk to the people you work with, and if you'd give them a chance, they'll love you too."

I stared at her. "Is that another compliment? Because we've just been through that."

She walked to her desk. "You mispronounced thank you."

Without responding, I pushed my office door open and went inside. I spent the next hour and fifty-five minutes going through the Kerual file, making notes and a report for my meeting. I was distracted though, with what Melinda had said. I'd avoided conversations with my co-workers for years because I didn't want them to think I was an idiot, and if I were being honest with myself, I did enjoy the brief conversation I'd had at lunch time. And if everyone decided to cook something once in a while and bring it to work to share, that had to be a good thing, right? And the fact was, now that I lived alone, the interaction with people was nice. Even if it was awkward and I made a fool of myself, I felt better for it. So just before I left for my two-o'clock, I emailed Melinda.

Thank you.

FRIDAY PASSED in a bit of blur. I had meetings, reports to do, and statistics to go over, and I was kept busy all day. I did notice the pretty red-haired girl that had spoken to me yesterday now smiled at me in the hall, and Lena and Kadin both greeted me with a "Hi Henry" as I entered the break room at lunchtime.

I was a little sore in the shoulders and quads from my workout the morning before, but it was what I'd call a pleasant soreness. It wasn't debilitating. It was just a gentle reminder that my body was changing, improving, and I liked that.

By the time I got home after work, going out for a drink with Anika was the last thing I felt like doing. Anika had texted me earlier to remind me, which was really a thinly veiled threat not to stand her up. So, like a good best friend, I dragged my arse into my closet and pulled out an outfit of dark jeans and a black sweater. I couldn't remember the last time I'd gone out. Certainly not with Graham. I preferred to spend my weekends staying in, having dinner parties, or quiet nights with a good book and a glass of wine. And I grumbled as I got changed, until I pulled on my jeans.

And holy shit. Not only were they not tight, but they were even a little big around the waist! I could do the button up easily with room to spare, and they were even a little roomy around my arse and thighs.

I walked out to look in the full-length mirror, a slow spreading smile covering my face.

Oh my God.

I hadn't noticed any change in my work pants. Well, they were a little loose, which I just fixed with a belt. I figured they were getting old or something. I didn't even think that much about it, to be honest. But this, these jeans, was proof that my change in diet and new exercise regime were working.

I grabbed my phone and thumbed to the camera. I took a picture of my reflection, with one hand pulling on the waistband of my jeans showing the extra room that wasn't there just three weeks ago. I quickly found Reed's number, attached the photo, and typed out an excited message.

Holy Crap, look at this!

His reply was almost immediate. *Excellent! Well done. I knew you could do it!*

I laughed at his reply. I don't think I'd smiled this much in weeks... *Sorry to bother you on a Friday night. Just wanted to share my excitement.*

It's no bother at all. Actually, you just made my day. Good to know all that hard work has paid off.

Are you saying I'm hard work?

I grinned at my phone, waiting for his reply. But instead of a message, my phone rang in my hand. Reed's name flashed on my screen, and I hit Answer, still smiling. There was no hello or anything. "Please tell me you were joking?"

"About me being hard work?"

"Yes!"

I laughed. "I was, yes. Though we both know I like to whinge a lot, and I complain about everything you make me do."

He laughed. It was a relieved sound. "Well, true. But you do whatever I make you do, no matter how much you know it will hurt."

"This is true. Never considered myself a masochist before. I'm actually rather enjoying the muscle soreness and twinges."

"Oh?"

"Yes, it reminds me that I'm doing something instead of sitting on my fat arse."

He chuckled. "You never had a fat arse."

"Well, these jeans beg to differ." I looked at myself in the mirror from a few different angles. "I haven't worn them in a while, and last time I did, they were a little snug."

"Well, you should be proud of yourself. These little milestones aren't so little, Henry. The last three weeks haven't been easy, but you've persevered and it's really starting to pay off."

"It is! Normally I would reward myself with cheesecake or something, but I might go for something different."

"Such as?"

"New gym clothes." It was an idea that came from nowhere, but once I'd said it out loud, I was keen to see it through. "The ones I've been wearing are the ones I bought years ago. Which you can probably tell."

"Clothes don't matter much to me."

I gasped, feigning shock and horror. "Are you even gay?"

He laughed. "Uh, yes. Very much."

"I was just kidding. Sort of. Clothes aren't *the* most important thing."

"Not like shoes."

"You like shoes?"

"No, I was taking the piss."

I gasped again. This time I wasn't faking the shock and horror so much. "I like shoes. Which reminds me, I should buy some new sneakers as well."

Reed laughed again. "Well, it's better than cheesecake."

"Well, we agree on that. Shoes *are* better than cheesecake. Barely."

"I've never had a sweet tooth," he admitted. "I'm more of a savoury kind of guy."

"I don't discriminate. I love all food. Which is probably why I was a hundred and fourteen kilos."

"Hey, I'm ninety-five kilos. Are you saying that's a lot?"

"Good Lord, no," I cried. "You're like a foot taller than me and have a body of a god. Ninety-five on you is perfect. Ninety-five is a dream for me."

There was a smile in his voice. "I was just kidding. I'm happy with where I'm at. And it won't take long for you. You'll notice clothes getting looser before a change in weight on the scales, so don't get caught up on numbers. Obsessing over scales isn't good for you. Feeling better and seeing how you look in the mirror and needing smaller clothes is a healthier gauge."

"You sound like you know what you're talking about."

He was silent a moment. "Yeah. I haven't always had— What did you call it? The body of a god?"

I laughed. I really did say that, didn't I? I wasn't even embarrassed. Much. "Okay, so maybe an Asgardian god, not a Greek god."

"Ah! Finally a movie reference I understand!" he said excitedly. "Wait. Am I like Thor or Loki?"

"Totally Thor."

"Oh, I prefer Loki, I think."

"Really? To be or to date? Because Thor in public and Loki in the bedroom would totally work for me."

Reed laughed long and loud. "I like the way you think."

I checked my watch. "Holy shit," I cried. I needed to finish getting ready but wasn't ready to say goodbye. "Hang on for a sec?" I didn't wait for his reply. I threw my phone onto my bed and pulled my sweater on and quickly donned some socks and my favourite boots. I freshened up in the bathroom the best I could and snatched up my phone. "You still there?"

"Yeah. Everything okay?"

"Oh sure. I just needed to finish getting ready. Anika will kill me if I'm late."

"Do you need to go?"

"Yes, well no, not really. I'm walking to the pub, so you wanna keep me company on the way there?" Shoving my keys in my front jeans pocket and wallet in the back, I pulled the front door shut behind me. The evening air was cooling off, and the busy Balmain street was humming with a Friday night buzz.

"Sure!"

"You can meet us there if you want?"

He paused, and I immediately regretted the invitation. "Nah, I'm already in my trackies in front of the TV, plus I've got an early start tomorrow. Maybe next time."

"Oh for sure," I said, trying to come off as cool or whatever. "So? What's for dinner tonight?"

"Baked sweet potato and grilled lamb steaks with a balsamic salad."

"Oh wow."

"Yeah, I love it. It's one of my favourites, and it's so easy."

"Is there some secret recipe, or is it as simple as it sounds?"

"I'll write you out the recipe. Or I could cook it for you one time." He swallowed hard. "If you want, that is?"

"Oh."

"Yeah well," he added quickly, "you brought some of that lemon tart in for me, so it's only fair I return the favour. I can bring some into the gym for you on Sunday."

"Or you could cook it for me." I almost tripped over my own feet on the footpath. I don't know what made me say that, but it sounded like that's what he meant, then tried to flounder his way out of it in case I said no. I didn't want him to feel bad. "I like my lamb cooked medium, thanks."

He chuckled warmly, a relieved sound. "I'll try to remember that."

"And I'll try and remember to bring another citrus tart."

He groaned, an almost obscene sound. "If you insist."

The guttural filthy hum reverberated from my ear down my spine, short-circuiting my brain. I did some kind of Mr Bean flail as I stepped out into Darling Street and was rewarded with a cacophony of curses and honks from traffic. I might have squealed.

Reed's voice was fast and concerned. "Henry, are you okay?"

"Oh sure," I replied, my free hand over my pounding heart. "Just sharing my awesome dance moves with oncoming traffic."

He snorted. "I'm pretty sure a car would win a dance off."

"Well, you've obviously never seen me dance, because that was a mix of Michael Jackson and Michael Flatley."

He snorted. "Sounds amazing."

"Of course it was. That's why they honked."

He burst out laughing. "You nearly at the pub yet?"

"Almost. A block to go." It was then I realised I wasn't out of breath, even after my River Dance with a car. "Huh. I think all that exercise nonsense you've been making me do is actually paying off. Not only do my jeans fit, but I'm not even puffing."

"Ah, there is method in the madness." There was a smile in his voice.

"Speaking of madness, what time do you start tomorrow?"

"Six."

"Jesus, ouch. That has to suck."

"It's not so bad."

"The same way that kale isn't so bad? Is there a kale scale? Like a Richter scale, only with the horrible nastiness that is kale? Kale would be an eight."

He chuckled. "Oh no, kale would be a six. Oysters would be an eight."

I nodded. "Agreed. I'll allow that. Nothing slimy and salty can taste good." I stopped in my tracks. "Well, that's not exactly true. Not *everything* that's salty and slimy is bad."

"I hear pineapple helps with that."

Now it was me who laughed. "I've heard that too, though I think it's a debunked urban myth."

"Did I miss an R rated episode of MythBusters?"

"You know, they really should have a sex version of that show."

"I'm pretty sure the Internet has it covered. Tumblr, Tinder, Grindr."

"I wouldn't know. I couldn't tell you the last time I tried dating. Oh good Lord, dating. Ugh. I'd prefer to eat an oyster and kale salad."

Reed laughed again. "Yeah, it's not easy."

"Have you dated much since... since you became single?"

"No, not really. A few times, but it never felt right. I dunno." He was quiet for a moment. "You must've arrived because I can hear people and music."

I was standing out the front of the hotel, not really wanting this conversation to end. I spotted Anika at a table, and she waved at me through the crowd. "Yeah, I'm here. And oh please help me, Anika has schnapps. This isn't going to end well."

He chuckled into the phone. "Sounds fun. Have a good night."

"Thanks for chaperoning me on my walk here."

"You're welcome."

"Have a good night."

"Same to you."

I disconnected my call and made my way inside and over to Anika. I kissed her cheek. "What's with the death wish so early in the evening for?" I asked, nodding toward the schnapps.

"Commiserating drinks?" She eyed me cautiously. "Which you don't apparently need."

"Why am I commiserating?" I racked my brain trying to think... Oh God. "Did Barry Gibb die?"

"No, I mean, we gave Graham until today and he didn't reply."

"Oh." Man, I'd not given that a thought. "I forgot about that."

Anika watched me for a long, scrutinising minute. She then noticed I was still holding my phone, and she took it from me. "Whoever you were talking to on the phone out there had you smiling," she said as she scrolled through my call list. "Jesus Henry. You were talking to Reed for an hour and twelve minutes!"

"We had things to discuss!"

"Such as?"

"Well, a few things... Thor, kale, and why gay men should eat pineapple."

Anika blinked, and a slow-spreading smile covered her face. "Are you and him...?"

"What? No! I told you before, he's so far out of my league it's ridiculous. And I'm not ready for that!"

She waved my phone in my face. "An hour and twelve minute phone call tells me otherwise."

I let out a long-suffering sigh, picked up my shot of schnapps, and downed it. Then, to prove my point, I picked up Anika's shot glass and downed it too.

And that pretty much sums up how my night went.

SEVEN

MY PHONE BEEPED, WAKING ME UP. I DIDN'T RECALL downloading an exploding jackhammer as my message sound, but it boomed in my head. I cracked one eye open and regretted it immediately. The blinding sunlight pierced my brain, spawning a thousand fire ants inside my skull.

Good. Fucking. Lord.

The thought of butterscotch schnapps made my stomach roll. And peach, and strawberry, and some glow in the dark glacier type of schnapps. *Fucking hell.*

I reached blindly for my phone hoping the message that woke me was from Anika and she was as sick as me, but when I could finally peel my eyelids open and focus on the screen, I saw it was Reed.

Did you survive?

My mouth felt like I'd licked the pavement the whole way home. Nausea bubbled in my stomach, and the fire ants were still partying in my head.

My replies were sent in separate, fragmented messages.

No.

Because schnapps.

Anika's fault.

#PrayForHenry

His reply was immediate. *HAHAHA*

Not funny. Dying.

Did you want to go shopping for new gym clothes?

Today?

Yes.

But I'm dying.

That bad, huh?

Spectacularly.

No worries.

Even hung-over I could tell he sounded disappointed. *Tomorrow? If I can manage being upright, I'll make you a citrus tart tonight.*

Deal. Will you be at your session with me in the morning?

Ugh, gym. How much would be a significant bribe to get me out of it?

Two citrus tarts.

I smiled, despite the pain in my head. *Did you know fire ants vomit lava?*

Um, that's random, but no I didn't know that.

True. They're inside my brain right now.

Vomiting lava?

Feels like it.

Oh, poor you.

I only have enough lemon butter for one citrus tart.

Then one will have to do.

I tried sitting up in bed and fell back with a groan. *Nope. Can't even sit up. I think fire ants vomit lava and wield tiny swords.*

LOL

Still not funny.

Go back to sleep Henry.

Thank you.

I rolled onto my side, threw my phone onto the bed beside me, and let the fire ants stab my brain.

———

I WALKED into the gym right on eight o'clock the next morning with my sunnies firmly in place. "Here he is," Reed greeted me cheerfully. "I wondered whether you would show today."

The lady at the counter with Reed, who I now knew to be Emily, smiled at me. "Reed told us about the hashtag Pray For Henry."

I nodded. "Did anyone hold a candlelight vigil for my brain cells that died?"

Reed snorted. "Should we have?"

"Yes."

"And what about the lava-vomiting, sword-wielding fire ants?" Reed asked.

"Evil little fuckers."

Reed and Emily both cracked up laughing. Then Reed asked, "Gonna take those sunglasses off?"

"I wasn't planning on it. Can I claim photosensitivity today?"

"Nope." Reed reached over, and using both hands, he gently removed my sunnies. Both he and Emily recoiled. "Ew."

"My eyeballs need cutting and bleeding."

Reed nodded. "Kinda. How did Anika pull up?"

"She still can't get out of bed."

Reed chuckled. "Must've been a good night."

"The last thing she remembers is me standing on a table and singing 'Drink With Me' from *Les Mis*." Reed laughed, and I cleared my throat. "Though I'm sure she's lying."

He was grinning now. "Mmhmm."

"'Can You Hear The People Sing' is by far a better a song

to sing while standing on a table. I'm pretty sure I'd have sung that. And it's so obvious that 'Empty Chairs' is only a song you sing at closing time."

Reed threw his head back and laughed. "So obvious."

"See? Everyone knows that."

"You have no recollection of singing?"

"None."

"Oh dear."

"Tell me about it."

"Then I better take it easy on you today."

"Yes, please."

I spent the next hour zoned out in some other mental space. Going through the motions of the treadmill, then the elliptical. I used the weights and pulley machine, upping my lift weight to fifteen kilos.

Reed was duly impressed. "You should be hung-over more often."

"I'm dying, just so you know."

He just grinned. "We still going gym clothes shopping? I need to get a new pair of jeans, and because I have no clue and you do, I thought we could do that while we're there too."

"Oh, sure. I'll go home first, though. I need to shower because I'm sweaty and gross." I was pretty sure my sweat smelled of schnapps. "You're done here in an hour?"

"Yep."

"When did you want me to bring you the citrus tart?"

His eyes lit up. "You made me one?"

"Of course."

"Oh, Henry. You *are* the best."

"I finally dragged myself out of bed at about four o'clock yesterday. I spent two hours trying to be upright and not dying in the shower, then when I could stand without dry heaving, I ordered Chinese food and made someone his new-favourite lemon dessert."

He was grinning, then he tilted his head. "Chinese food for a hangover?"

"Wonton soup. The right mix of salty and sweet, liquid and food, all in the one dish."

"I'm more of a burger and Coke kind of guy."

"You? A burger and Coke? Does that not breach every dietary rule you have?"

"Only for hangovers. And let's face it, the alcohol the night before has pretty much killed the diet. Saturated fat and sodium and a tonne of sugar are the only things that will fix me. Not that I drink that often. And when I do drink, I don't inhale schnapps."

"Ugh. Don't even say that word."

"My grandmother is German," Reed said wistfully. "She has the real schnapps if you want me to hook you up?"

I squinted at him. "I think that citrus tart just became mine."

He laughed. "I'll see you out the front in about an hour."

———

I PULLED up at the gym and had to wait a few minutes. I was contemplating sending him a quick text when he came through the front doors, laughing at something or with someone inside. When he got into the car, his reason for being a little late was obvious. He smelled of soap and deodorant, and his hair was damp and neatly brushed.

I wasn't sure which I preferred: fresh and clean or hot and sweaty. I shook that thought from my head. "You showered?"

He stuffed his gym bag by his feet. "Yep. I didn't want to be trying on clothes straight after work. I'm sure there are health regulations against being sweaty and gross and putting on clothes someone else might buy." He clicked his seatbelt on, settled in comfortably with a grin, while impossibly filling one half of my car with his huge frame. "Were you waiting long?"

"No, not at all. I was busy selling your citrus tart on eBay to the highest bidder."

Reed looked at me like I'd just flicked a little puppy on the head. I may have laughed.

"Oh, I see how it is." He shook his head and chuckled at me. "So, where are we going to?"

"I was thinking Birkenhead. Is that okay with you? Or would you prefer the city?" Birkenhead Point was a huge factory outlet shopping centre with everything imaginable, from a dollar shop to Ralph Lauren. But it was kind of close, and I knew he rode his bike there often, and given he didn't have a car and I was driving, he might prefer a trip to the city. "I have a parking spot in the city. Let's go there."

Reed shrugged, like he really didn't care either way. "Okay."

The beauty of living in Balmain was that it was literally a ten-minute drive into the city. I pulled into my work car park, which took us about four storeys below Pitt Street. When we'd finally circled down and I drove into a reserved spot with my number plate painted on the wall, Reed seemed surprised. "You do this every day?"

"Yep. Though sometimes if I know I'll be finishing early, I'll leave the car at home and jump on a bus." I pointed over to the elevator, and we walked toward it. "Traffic today was great. Weekdays aren't always so good."

"I'll never complain about my short stroll to work again."

We stepped into the elevator, and I pressed the button to the street level. "Yeah, you've got it pretty easy."

"Except when it rains."

"What do you do when it rains?"

"Get wet."

I snorted. "Nice."

"Well, see, they have these new inventions nowadays called umbrellas."

I rolled my eyes. "Yeah okay. Hey, would you look at that?" I said, pulling out my phone. "The highest bidder of the lemon tart just won."

Reed laughed as we stepped out of the elevator and into Martin Place and into the warm Sydney sun. The sky was blue, people walking past were smiling, and I had to wonder when the last time I stopped to consider if it was a nice day or not.

"So you work along here?" Reed asked.

"Yep. Just down there," I said, pointing to the huge sandstone heritage building. "But it's not that exciting."

"Well, not for you," he countered. "But it's a pretty special place to work, no?"

I smiled up at him. "I guess."

"Though I don't envy you the corporate uniform."

"I actually don't mind wearing a suit every day. It eliminates the dilemma of what to wear."

Reed scoffed. "Yeah, no thanks. Give me my gym shorts and T-shirt any day. Though I've seen you in your suit. Very suave."

I remembered when I'd delivered the slice of lemon tart to the gym on my way to work the other day. He'd waved, so that's when he must have seen me. "Do you think flattery will get you your citrus tart back? Because the guy on eBay put in a pretty good offer."

He chuckled warmly. "The flattery is real, but I'll shout you a coffee as bribery for the tart."

"Mmm, flattery and coffee. Two of my favourite things."

Reed gave me his award-winning smile, and as we walked down George Street toward the Strand, I learned he grew up in Leichhardt, has one brother and two sisters, his parents are still happily married, he has a huge extended family of nieces and nephews, cousins, aunts and uncles, and if I could possibly imagine an Australian-German comedy and food festival, that about summed up his family. Or so he said.

I explained my family was probably the opposite. "My dad left when I was four. I don't remember him. My mum did a great job raising my sister and me on her own. I have two cousins in Melbourne, well, I think that's where they still live. I'm not particularly close to my sister, though we get on well enough I suppose. And to give you a likeness of my family, I'd have you watch an episode of *Mrs Brown's Boys*."

Reed burst out laughing. "Sounds entertaining."

"Well, Christmas is always interesting. And mildly disturbing."

We hit the sportswear store first, and I couldn't hide my smile when I actually tried on and bought two new pair of shorts and two shirts in a smaller size. I chose a pair of new sneakers that matched both outfits, and I left the store happier than I'd been in a long time.

Holding my bag of shopping like an Oscar, I gave a speech worthy of one——if they gave Oscars for really bad American actor impersonations. "I'd like to thank my personal trainer, Reed. I'd like to thank my mom and all my fans. I couldn't do this without you."

Reed laughed as he pushed me out of the store. "You crack me up."

"You're welcome! Now, let's find you some jeans." I looked up the Strand in both directions, not sure which way to go. "So, where does a six-foot-three body builder buy his jeans?"

"JeansForGiants.com normally, but they were all out of the body builder's fit."

Now it was me who laughed. "That's unfortunate."

He rolled his eyes at me. "I dunno, let's try an everyday jeans store for everyday people? And I'm not a body builder.

I'm a personal trainer, which you correctly addressed me as in your Emmy Award winning speech back there."

"It was the Oscars, and yes, I stand corrected. You are a personal trainer, and a very good one at that." I hoped he saw the sincerity in my face. "And I meant what I said. I couldn't have done this without you. I'd still be fat and single, crying in my cheesecake if it weren't for you." Then I amended, "Well, I'm still fat and single, but I haven't had cheesecake in three weeks. That's gotta be some kind of record."

Reed stopped walking, and when I turned to face him, he wasn't smiling. "Don't call yourself fat."

"It's true though."

"You're more than a label, Henry," he said quietly. "Someone else's label, I might add. Just because what's-his-name——"

"Voldemort."

"Just because Voldemort is a short-sighted, superficial arse-hole, doesn't mean you are what he says you are."

A short-sighted, superficial arsehole. Right then. "Jeez, Reed. Tell me how you really feel about him."

"I'm sorry, but if he can't see the real you, he doesn't deserve the real you."

I fought a smile. "Oh no, you were right the first time. He is a superficial arsehole."

Reed laughed at himself then shook his head. "I am sorry. I shouldn't have said that. But I have issues with words like fat."

I'd never seen such a tall and intimidating guy look so vulnerable. I guessed working in the fitness industry, it was only natural that Reed was more aware of body image issues. "I'm sorry too. I didn't mean anything by it."

"Nah, it's alright." He shrugged it off. "Are we good?"

"Yes, of course. Well, not entirely. You still haven't bought me that coffee yet."

He rewarded me with that perfect smile. "Jeans or coffee first?"

"Whichever shop we pass first."

"Deal."

We walked up to the Pitt Street Mall and found us a jeans shop first. And I had to admit, going jeans shopping with Reed wasn't exactly a hardship. Except for the sales guy, who just about fell over himself trying to help him. Some bottle-blond twink with twigs for legs and zero shame pounced on Reed like a Chihuahua trying to hump his leg.

"Oh, you'd look great in these," Chihuahua boy yipped. He looked Reed up and down and grabbed a pair of jeans from the display and gave them to him. "These would fit you like a glove." I wasn't sure if he was going for seductive, but the deliberate finger stroke on Reed's hand made me want to smack the kid on the nose with a rolled up newspaper.

Reed took a small step back from him. "Uh, thanks." He glanced at me and smiled with a "please help" look in his eyes. "Can you hold them for me, babe?"

Babe? What the...?

Reed narrowed his eyes at me and gave a quick pointed nod toward Chihuahua boy. *Oh, right.* "Sure," I said cheerfully, taking the folded jeans from Chihuahua boy. He looked me up and down with a sour look on his face. I'm pretty sure he didn't fall for it. I mean, Reed was something straight out of *Fitness Gods*, and I was... well, I was me.

"If we need any help, I'll let you know," Reed said, dismissing him with a charming smile. Reed quickly snatched up a few pairs of different jeans, grabbed my hand, and led me to the back of the store to the change rooms. When we were out of view from Chihuahua boy, Reed dropped my hand and sighed. "I'm sorry about that."

"Don't worry about it," I said, trying to play it cool. My hand was still tingling from his touch.

Reed let out a frustrated sound. "It pisses me off when that happens."

"Happens a lot, does it?"

He rolled his eyes. "Sorry."

"Don't apologise. It's not your fault the twinky Chihuahua tried to hump your leg."

Reed finally started to smile. "Chihuahua?"

I nodded. "His full pedigree kennel name is Shameless Bottom Needs a Muscle Daddy, but he gets called Chihuahua Boy for short."

Reed stared at me for a second before he burst out laughing. Like *really* laughed, *really* loudly. Even when he'd gone into one of the change rooms, he was still chuckling. I stood by his door, and when he opened it and stepped out, he was still smiling. "What about these?"

Reed stood there with the dark denim jeans on, with bare feet, holding his shirt up a little so I could see the waistband. And those damn V muscles that framed his hips and a trail of dark brown hair that ran from his navel and disappeared under the button of his jeans...

Jeans. Right. Yes, he's wearing jeans. That's what we're doing here.

"How do they feel?" I asked, pretending not to have noticed his body.

He bent one leg at the knee to stretch them and stuck his thumb under the waistband. "They feel good." Then he turned around to show me the back. And the way they framed his arse...

Fucking hell.

"Well, they look like they were made for you."

He gave me an honest, eye-crinkling smile. "Next pair," he said before disappearing back into the change room.

I resisted the urge to fan my face, though I'm sure I was flushed. I mean, I hadn't been physically attracted to someone in a long time. Well, of course I had been attracted to Graham, but the passion between us in the bedroom had died off years ago.

God, how blind was I to the state of my relationship with him?

The change room door opened, startling me. And I hadn't noticed Chihuahua boy come in either. The sales guy was standing there, staring at Reed. "What about these?" Reed asked.

I could tell by the look on his face he didn't like them, but before I could answer, Blondie McLeghumper spoke. "Oh, they look good." Of course he'd say that. The jeans Reed was trying on were the same as he was wearing.

Reed was still barefoot and holding his shirt up a little so his perfectly sculptured waist was in full view. The jeans were tight, clearly outlining the muscle definition in his thighs and calves, not to mention the pronounced bulge in his groin. If it were possible to spray on jeans, these were it. Mr Platinum Droolerboy was two seconds away from stripping naked and launching himself at Reed. *Jesus, did he just purr?*

Reed looked at me for help. "They don't suit you," I said. "Not your style at all. You'd never be comfortable in those."

He looked right at me and smiled. "You're right." He stepped back into the change room and shut the door. "Next pair!"

I turned to face the sales assistant, who was staring, dazed and slack-jawed, at Reed's change room door. He seemed to have forgotten where he was, and it took him a moment to look at me. I slowly raised my bitch brow at him, which Anika once said could level the bravest of men, and I watched as he paled. I didn't really want this to become a bottom-bitch fight, but I had this guy beat. I mean, I had fifteen years on him at least: I had mastered the "back the fuck off from my man" look when this kid was still in nappies.

He gave me a weak smile and retreated, wandering off to another customer, and it occurred to me that maybe Reed wanted to meet someone new. It also occurred to me that I'd just thought of Reed as *my man*.

Which he wasn't. Friend, maybe. Boyfriend, definitely not.

I wasn't ready for that.

Reed opened the door and stepped out. "What about these?"

I stared at his face, not even looking at his jeans. "Did you want...? Are you interested in him because I——"

"What?"

"Chihuahua b—— I mean the sales assistant guy."

Reed looked horrified. He pointed out into the store and whispered, "That guy?"

I nodded.

Reed balked at first then laughed. "Uh no. No. No. He's not my type."

I let out a breath of relief. "Oh, thank God. I didn't think so, because you called me babe in front of him, but I thought I should ask. I mean, I just sent him packing with my bitch brow, and I thought maybe I shouldn't have."

"Your bitch brow?"

"Yeah, you know..." I gave him a demonstration, waving at my face like it was on *The Price is Right*.

He made a pained ooooh face. "I see."

I nodded. "I should probably apologise," I said, looking out to where the sales guy had gone.

Reed just laughed. "Oh, Henry. Don't worry about him." He chuckled for a while then turned around and lifted his shirt to show off his arse. "How about these?"

"Very nice." Then I actually looked at the jeans. "Yeah, they're great. How do they feel?"

He bent each leg at the knee again, which was apparently the Reed gauge of denim flexibility. "Mmm."

"You like the first pair best," I stated.

"What do you think?"

"I think the first pair were better too."

He smiled again and disappeared back into the change room. When he was done, he paid for his jeans, and the sales guy had lost a little of his sparkle. Well, he was still smarmy and desperate, and he was giving Reed serious bedroom eyes, but Reed just thanked him and we left.

When we started walking back up the mall, Reed gave me a sad smile. "Thank you for playing along with the whole 'babe' thing. I thought if he knew we were together, he'd back off."

"Oh, that's fine. No problem. He was keen, that's for sure. Did you see how he was looking at you when he was serving you just now?"

Reed visibly shuddered. "This might sound conceited, but it happens more than I'd like to admit, and I hate it. At first it was flattering, now it's just awkward. And some guys don't get the message. I guess they assume most gay guys are up for a quickie or whatever." He blushed a little. "But that's not my style."

"Mine either," I admitted. "Not that guys hit on me like that. I don't exactly have that problem."

"Ah, that's because you haven't made them your citrus tart."

I snorted. "Oh yeah, it brings all the boys to the yard."

Reed laughed, and then right there in the middle of the Pitt Street Mall, a Hellmouth opened. "Henry?"

Oh no. I knew that voice...

Reed turned to the sound of my name being called, but I froze. I wasn't ready for this.

"Henry?"

I turned this time to find Colin and James, Graham's best friends. They were good friends of mine too, up until three weeks ago.

"Colin, James," I said in greeting.

They each gave me an awkward hug. "How are you?" Colin asked.

"Good. And you?" I couldn't keep the chill from my tone.

"We're good," Colin replied.

James nodded but couldn't take his eyes off Reed. "Hi," James said, looking from Reed to me, expecting an introduction.

"Hi," Reed answered shortly. He clearly picked up on my discomfort.

"We better get going," I said quickly. I wasn't giving them anything. "Or we'll be late."

Colin seemed to get it. "Okay. It's good to see you, Henry. You look great." He gave me a sad smile. "For what it's worth, I'm sorry about what happened. Graham's——"

I put my hand up. "Don't. I don't want to know."

"Fair enough," Colin said. "Sorry."

I looked up at Reed. "You ready?"

He gave a nod, and we turned to head back up toward Martin Place. We'd only walked a few metres when Reed asked, "You okay?"

I nodded. "They were good friends but chose Graham in the split. Well, they were his friends first."

"Collateral damage, huh?"

I nodded, and he quickly looked over his shoulder back to where Colin and James were. "They're still watching," Reed said and put his arm around my shoulder as we walked. "This okay?"

The weight of his arm, the warmth, the contact, felt really good. "Yeah."

"You pretended to be my boyfriend in the store to help me," Reed said. "Just returning the favour."

"Are they still watching?" I asked.

He looked back again and smiled. "Yep."

"James is probably calling Graham right now."

Reed was quiet for a few steps. "Do you want him to?"

"Call Graham?" I repeated. "I don't care."

Reed stopped walking, and with his arm still around my shoulders, he turned me so we stood facing each other. His hand now rested gently near my neck. "You do care. And that's what makes you a better person than him. Because he can't even return a text message. So let him not care, because he's an arsehole. But you're not. It's okay to care, Henry. I like that you still care."

"Of course I care," I admitted. "I always will. But not like that. Not anymore."

"What do you mean?"

"I don't know what I feel for him. I'm not hurt and angry anymore. I should be, but I'm not. And I have to wonder what that means."

Just then, a far off, very familiar voice yelled out. "Henry?"

Oh dear God. You've got to be kidding me.

"Henry?"

I slowly closed my eyes and wondered if clicking my heels together three times and saying, "There's no place like home," would actually work. I opened my eyes to find I wasn't Dorothy, and I was in fact still in Pitt Street. I put my hand on Reed's arm. "Run for your life," I whispered.

He stared at me with wide eyes. "Why?"

"Henry! Yoohoo!"

My shoulders sagged, and I could feel my soul being sucked out of my body. There was no escaping it. I sighed, resigned, and turned to face my accuser. "Mum!"

I should've realised. It was Sunday; we were out the front

of the Nespresso shop. My mother was dressed to the nines. My sister was with her. I kissed them both on the cheek. "George Clooney a no-show again?"

My mother sighed dramatically. "It's false advertising. He's there on the ads." She looked up at Reed and smiled deliriously. "Now Henry, where are your manners? And who is this nice boy with his hand on you?"

Reed dropped his hand, and I withheld a sigh. "Yes, mum this is Reed. Reed, this is my mother, Rosemary, and my sister, Eadie."

Both women stared up at him and smiled. Reed nodded politely. "Hello. Nice to meet you." I gave him my best "I'm so sorry" eyes, but he just smiled like it was all the most natural thing in the world.

"Reed and I were just leaving," I blurted out.

"Oh, that's a shame," my mother said. Then she gave me a once over. "Henry, you look great!"

"Well, you can thank Reed for that," I said.

"I bet we can," Eadie said with a sly smile.

I glared at her. "Not like that. He's been helping me with my fitness."

"I bet he has," Eadie said, still smiling up at Reed. "Never really liked Graham much."

"Eadie," I warned. "Don't you have another wedding to plan or something?"

"Oh, cut it out you two," Mum said. Then she frowned at me and put her hand on my arm. "I'm sorry about how things went with Graham. But you do look really good, Henry. You haven't come over for dinner since you broke up with him. I haven't seen you in weeks."

"I've been busy," I lied.

"That's no excuse, Henry," Mum chastised. Then she looked at Reed. "He should've at least called me. I've been so worried."

"Yes, Henry," Reed agreed with a smirk. "You should have."

I shot him a quick glare then smiled perfectly at my mother. "We really do have to get going. I'll call you, I promise."

I kissed them both on the cheek again and pretty much dragged Reed away by the arm. "It was nice to meet you," he called out, and they stood there smiling at him and waving like schoolgirls with crushes.

"God, I'm so sorry," I said as we hurried away.

"Why?" He looked amused by the whole thing. "Is there anyone else you'd like to run into today?"

"No thanks. I'm done for the year."

"Not even George Clooney?" Reed asked. "Does your mum honestly think he'll be at the Nespresso store because he's on the ads on TV?"

I laughed at that. "She does. She's even written letters to complain that it's false advertising. Which is horribly embarrassing. But according to her, he'll only be there on Sundays. God knows why. Actually, I think it's a religious thing."

"I can see that," Reed said. He clearly thought the whole thing was funny. "The Church of George. Makes perfect sense to me."

"Ah, so George's your type?"

He glanced sidelong at me.

I quickly clarified, "Well, the guy at the gym wasn't your type. The sales clerk in the jeans store wasn't your type..."

We turned into Martin Place, and Reed still hadn't answered. He smiled kind of awkwardly and said, "Your mum and sister seem really nice."

Okay then. Types were off the discussion list. "You know, I'll never hear the end of her seeing me with your hand on my shoulder. My mother will now ask about you until the day I die."

Reed just laughed. "I'm sure it won't be that bad."

"Oh, it will be. She'll have us married by dinner time."

He chuckled at that. "She was concerned about you."

"Yeah, I know." I shrugged one shoulder. "When Graham left I let her know, and she wanted me to come around for dinner. But I didn't want to relive the whole thing over again, and the sympathy and pity... you know how that is."

"Yeah, I get that."

"But I will. I'll call her this week and arrange something. Though now I'll get to play Three Dozen Questions about you."

"Just do what I do," he said. "Tell them all the sex details, and believe me, they stop asking."

I cracked up laughing. "Did you really?"

He nodded proudly. "Yep. I got sick of the nosey questions, so I didn't hold back. And we're a pretty open family, but after explaining the mechanics of gay sex just once no one has asked me anything since."

By the time I stopped laughing, we were almost back to the elevator to the underground parking. "Hey," I said. I turned around and looked back down Martin Place. "I've just walked half the CBD, and I'm not even out of breath! And not even that, I feel like I could do it ten times over!"

Reed's smile was genuine. "That's great, Henry. Soon you'll be doing the Bay Run!"

"Pfft. Not likely."

"Why not?"

"Because I've seen the people who do the Bay Run. They're all super fit, crazy people."

"Hey, I do the Bay Run."

"No offence."

He smiled. "None taken. But you could totally manage it. You don't have to run the whole way. Most people walk some, jog some."

"I almost die doing a three kilometre walk on a treadmill."

"The Bay Run's only seven K," he countered. He looked ominously cheerful and nodded like he'd decided something. "I'm going to work your training schedule around getting you ready for a Bay Run."

"Against my consent. Isn't that against the Geneva Convention or something?"

"I'll double check the human rights handbook when I get home, but I'm pretty sure you signed a waiver."

"I signed a waiver in case I died."

"Then if you die on the Bay Run, I'll be covered."

My mouth fell open. Then I sniffed and pretended to open an imaginary envelope. "And the personal trainer of the year award goes to...."

Reed laughed. "You're welcome."

I thumped the elevator door button. "I'm not sure."

"It'll be a few weeks away, Henry. You'll have plenty of time to be ready," he added. "I wouldn't suggest it if I didn't think you were capable." The elevator doors opened and we stepped inside. "I'll do it with you."

I chewed the inside of my lip, still not convinced. "I don't know..."

"It'll be fun!"

"I think you need a dictionary because that's not what fun means. Running seven kilometres is torture. Of the cardiovascular kind."

The elevator doors opened, and we headed toward my car. "I can get you into a cardio-aerobic class if you like?"

Okay, he'd officially lost his mind. "Like the Olivia Newton John 80s music video?"

He laughed, and the sound echoed throughout the underground car park. "You don't have to wear leg-warmers if you don't want."

I lifted my chin. "Maybe I want to wear them."

"So you'll do it?"

"What? The Bay Run, or 'Let's Get Physical' dance moves?"

"Both."

I cringed. "Why do I feel like I'll end up doing both whether I want to or not?"

Reed grinned victoriously. "Excellent."

I pressed the unlock button on my car and threw my new purchases into the back. "Hey!"

"Hey what?"

"You never bought me a coffee! That was part of our deal!"

He looked genuinely sorry. "I forgot! We can go back up if you want?"

"No, it's fine. I can always email that eBay buyer and ask if he still wants the lemon tart."

Reed rolled his eyes, but he was smiling. "Wow. You play mean."

I got into the driver's seat and waited for Reed to contort his huge body into the passenger side before I started the car. "Yes, I do. It's part of my charm."

"That's okay, though, because I got you doing a gym cardio class *and* the Bay Run."

And as we made our way back up to street level and out into the easy Sunday traffic, my phone rang. Of course Bluetooth picked it up and the call came through the speakers of the car. It was Anika, and without really thinking, I hit Answer. "Hi."

"Oh hey," she replied. "Are you driving?"

"Yes. And you're on speaker, and Reed's in the car."

There was a beat of silence, and that was when I truly regretted taking her call. "Oh." I could tell she was smiling. "Hello, Reed."

He looked at me and half-frowned, half-smiled. "Uh, hi."

"Where have you guys been?" she asked slowly. She was still smiling, I could tell.

"In the city," I answered, commandeering the conversation. "And I ran into Colin and James."

"Oh man."

"And my mother and Eadie."

Anika laughed. Really loudly. "Did you break a mirror or walk under a ladder this morning or something?"

"You'd think so."

"How was it?" she asked.

"Awful. Horrifically embarrassing."

"It wasn't that bad," Reed added. "James and Colin might be under the impression that Henry and I are dating."

More silence. Then a bubble of laughter burst through the speakers. "What?"

"It's a long story," I said quickly. "I'll tell you about it later."

"Henry Ashford Beckett," Anika full-named me. "You tell me about it now."

Reed snorted. "Ashford? Is that your middle name?"

"Yes."

"Ouch."

Anika laughed, and I sighed. "It was my mother's maiden name. Both Eadie and I have the same middle name." It was something I'd explained numerous times in my life. "I didn't actually pick it. You can blame my mother."

Reed seemed to be enjoying this. "And Henry's mother might possibly think we're an item. She wants us married by dinner time, is that right, Henry?"

"Oh shut up," I cried. Anika was still laughing. "You're obviously feeling better. Not hung-over anymore?"

"Much better thanks," she said. "So tell me? You guys spent another day together. Colin and James *and* your mother all think something's going on——"

"Nothing's going on," I blurted out. I could feel my face heat with embarrassment. "I'm ending this call now, Anika."

Her response was shrill and fast. "Are you two fucking?"

I stabbed the End Call button on the dash screen, hard and repeatedly. I was too scared to look at Reed, but I could feel him staring at me, and when I finally dared to meet his gaze, his smile got wider and he burst out laughing. "I like Anika," he said.

"I don't. And just so you know, I'm now in the market for a new best friend because she just got fired. I'm so sorry about that. She has no filter, which is ultimately why we get on so well, but——"

"Henry?"

"Yes?"

"It's fine."

"Ugh. Today's been horrible for you. First Colin and James, then my mother and sister, *then* Anika. All I can do is apologise."

"I actually had fun today. It certainly wasn't horrible. Awkward, maybe, but not horrible."

"Oh God, awkward is worse than horrible."

Reed chuckled. "It wasn't bad! I've had a great day!"

I took a right into Darling Street at Balmain and drove past the gym and went straight to my place. When I stopped the car, Reed looked a little surprised and started to collect his shopping bags. "What are you doing?" I asked.

"I can walk from here. It's fine."

"You're not walking home from here," I said. "Just let me grab the citrus tart for you, and I'll drive you home."

"Oh." He smiled. "Okay."

From the way he bit his lip and blushed a little, I couldn't work out whether he was embarrassed or relieved or nervous. I ducked inside, quickly grabbing the tart, and when I got back into my car, I handed it straight to him. "Your bribery, paid in full."

He grinned at it. "Well, I think it was supposed to be two, but I'll settle for one."

"Oh please." I scoffed. "You owe me coffee and that lamb and sweet potato salad. Don't think I've forgotten."

"Yeah, right," Reed said softly. And he was quiet after that. Only when I pulled the car into his allocated parking spot, he swallowed hard. "Did you want to come inside?" He licked his lips nervously. "I can make you that coffee, and we can share this."

I wasn't sure what he was asking. Inviting someone in for coffee was an old cliché for sex——well, it used to be, the last time I played the whole dating game, but surely Reed was just being polite. I did mention that he owed me a coffee, so maybe I made him feel guilty. "Um," I started, unsure of what he really meant, therefore unsure of how to answer.

"You don't have to, of course. I just..." He bit his lip and shrugged.

The thing was, I would otherwise go home to an empty house. And I'd had a great day with him. I truly enjoyed his company, and for some absurd reason, he seemed to enjoy mine. Did I want to spend more time with him? "Sure," I finally answered. "I'd love to."

EIGHT

REED'S APARTMENT WAS KIND OF SMALL, BUT I guessed that was a given for a one-bedroom unit. It was spotlessly clean, with polished pine floorboards, white walls, and a newish kitchen. He had a peacock-blue sofa that matched an abstract print on the wall, a large flat screen TV, and a coffee table. His place smelled like him, and he was clearly very comfortable in his own space. He dumped his shopping bag on his small dining table, then added his keys and wallet. He took the citrus tart from me. "Take a seat."

He walked into the kitchen, which was just off the living and dining area, and called out to me. "You can turn the telly on. Bathroom's down the hall on your left, if you need."

"Thanks." I went over to the sofa and fell into it. It was as comfy as it looked.

I could hear beeping of some kind, which I assumed was a coffee machine, when Reed came out holding two small pods. "Strong or mild coffee?"

"Strong, please."

He disappeared again and I had a brief moment of "what the hell am I doing?" when I noticed a book on his coffee table. It was *Harry Potter and the Goblet of Fire* with a take-away menu slotted in as a bookmark.

I'd given Reed the first Harry Potter book the other week-end, and now he was almost finished with the fourth? That made me happier than it probably should've, and it kind of eased my doubts of why I was there. As strange as it was, this *was* the reason I was there. I gave him one book, and he read three more. He pushed me in the gym, getting more from me than I thought possible, and I still had more to offer. He gave me some lemon butter, and two citrus tarts later, I was in his living room for coffee.

We got on well. But more than that, we were productive together, and I really liked that.

"I blame you for that," he said, coming up behind me with two coffee cups in his hands and nodding to the Harry Potter book in my hand. He put them on the coffee table and turned to walk back into the kitchen. "I read the first one you gave me, then had to buy the others." He came back with two small plates this time and handed one to me. It was a triangle of the citrus tart and a spoon. "They're pretty good." He sat on the sofa with me and delicately cut into the dessert with his spoon and tasted it. And he groaned that guttural sound, low and filthy and pure sex, and I was pretty sure I'd do anything to hear it again. "Oh man, that is really good."

I shoved a spoonful into my mouth to distract me from where my thoughts had taken me, and I had to admit, the citrus tart was pretty good. "No wonder everyone at work liked it." I explained how everyone who had tried my morning tea then spoke to me.

"And it's really the first time you've spoken to anyone you work with in all the time you've been there?"

"I speak to them," I admitted. "About work related matters. Never anything personal, and never more than a hello in the hallway. But anyway, this new Monday morning tea is becoming quite the thing. Everyone's getting in on it. Last week, Rebecca from Insurance brought in a pear and raspberry bread. And Bayram from Corporate brought in homemade baklava. There was a mix up about whose turn it was, not that anyone minded because we had two morning teas. Anyway, it was all to die for. I only had a tiny bit of each, but it's been nice. Actually speaking to the people I work with about non-work related things."

"I find it a bit weird that you don't talk to them," he said, now sipping his coffee. "I thought you'd be friends with all of them."

"Friends with Melinda, yes. I adore her. Even though I'm technically her boss, she has no qualms in telling me to shut up or to pull my head in."

"Pretty sure I'd like her."

I nodded. "I'm sure you would."

He finished the last of his tart and slid his plate onto the coffee table. He sipped his coffee again. He was so relaxed and natural. I envied how comfortable he was in his own skin. "I love the people I work with," he said. "We all know each other's stories, their friends and families. Admittedly, there's only five of us full-time, not like the fifty or so that I guess work in your department. But even the part-timers and casual staff at the gym are all good people. I do get on with Emily the best, though, and Lachie. They'd be my closest friends."

I'd seen both Emily and Lachie around the gym all the time. They were always helpful and polite. I could see why he liked them. "They seem like nice people."

"We're doing an instructor challenge this weekend," he said, his face lighting up. "On Saturday afternoon. You should come and watch."

"What exactly is an instructor challenge?"

"All the trainers are set a routine, and whoever finishes first, wins. Sometimes it'll be whoever does more reps in a set time frame wins. We don't know what the challenge is going to be until we get there."

I stared at him. "You mean, exercise for fun?"

Reed laughed. "It is fun! You should come watch. I'm gonna win this time."

"How often do you do these?"

"Every couple of months."

"You're all crazy."

"It's pretty intense."

"And it's this Saturday?"

"Yep. At three o'clock." He put his cup back on the table. "Did you have something else planned?"

"Nope. I don't think so. I've renounced Anika's best friend status, remember? Though I might take my mum out for a brunch. That'll keep her happy for a while. I should be free in the afternoon."

"Excellent!"

"And you're really going to make me do the Bay Run?"

"Yep."

"You don't have to be so cheerful about trying to kill me."

He chuckled. "You'll be surprised how easy you'll do it."

"What? The dying part? Sure, that's easy. It's the running part that's hard."

He smiled as he leaned back in the sofa. "I'll redo your training schedule. It was due to be redone soon anyway."

"Why redo it? I was just getting the hang of it. I could just get through the whole session without wanting to die."

"That's why I need to change it."

"So you are trying to kill me?"

Reed smiled warmly at me. "You're improving. You need more of a challenge to push yourself."

"Can't I just plateau out at mediocre?"

He chuckled at that, then fell quiet, though he never took his eyes off me. "Nope. You're far from mediocre, Henry." His eyes were so intense, his gaze seemed to charge the air between us. The static surprised me. He shook his head a little and shot to his feet and quickly cleared the plates from the coffee table. "I'll just take these..." he mumbled, disappearing into his kitchen.

I let out a slow and steady breath. *What the fuck was that?* If I didn't know better, I could have sworn that was a *look*. But I did know better. He was popular, friends with everyone, gorgeous, with a body to die for. And I was... none of those things.

I'd been kicked off the couple train and left at the station for the old and overweight just three weeks ago. After eight years.

My head kept saying I wasn't ready for this. I needed time to be myself again. I needed to rediscover who I was as an individual person, not as part of a couple. I needed to learn how to be alone and to be okay with that.

But my heart was pretty sure I'd spent most of the last eight years alone. My heart was yearning for something it had been deprived of for far too long.

And I didn't know what to make of that.

How could I have spent the last eight years with someone and feel alone? How could I find myself suddenly single and there be no void where Graham had been? I didn't even realise how alone I was until he was gone, because it was only after he'd left me that I realised my life wasn't that much different.

The saying "you don't know what you've got until it's gone" was opposite for me. I was only now realising what I was missing out on, now that he was gone.

So maybe Graham saw that all along. We were so stagnant, so comfortable with each other, we were holding each other back. We were just numb with the status quo, and I could see that now. As hard as it was to admit, Graham had done the right thing.

So what did Reed have to do with that? I wasn't sure...

"Want another coffee?" Reed's voice snapped me out of my thoughts. He was standing in the doorway to his kitchen, putting a very deliberate distance between us.

"No," I answered, standing up. "I should get going."

Reed wiped the palms of his hands down his thighs. "Oh, okay." He swallowed hard, clearly uncomfortable now. "Hey, thanks for today. I had a great time."

"No worries. Thank you for not freaking out when we met my old friends. And my mother. And then Anika on the phone..." The corner of my mouth pulled down. "For all of it really. Maybe next time we can go somewhere where I don't know anyone."

He finally smiled. "Next time?"

"Yeah, if you want to, that is." *God, why couldn't I stop talking?*

He nodded. "Sure. I'd like that. Don't forget next Saturday though, be at the gym at three."

"Oh for sure. And you still have to make me that lamb and sweet potato salad. Don't think I've forgotten."

He smiled more naturally now. It suited him so much better. "Deal."

I walked to his front door. "Thanks again. See you Tuesday morning?"

He stood about a metre from me, his hands shoved in his pockets. "I'll be there."

I wouldn't say it was awkward, but there was something there. Something electric, something frightening, something that both thrilled me and terrified me.

With a clumsy smile, I opened the door and walked to my car. I hadn't even started the engine before I had Anika on the phone. She answered my call with, "You hung up on me."

"You embarrassed me."

"Henry, what's wrong?"

"I just left Reed's place."

"Oh my God. Did you sleep with him?"

"What? No!"

"You should. You need a newly-single fuck."

"Anika!"

She was silent for a long moment. "Oh my God, Henry..."

I nodded, even though she couldn't see. "I know."

"You like him."

"I don't know. I think so? How is that possible?"

I heard her mumble something like her hand was covering the phone. Then she said, "We'll be around for dinner. Cook us something nice, Henry."

And the line was dead. I drove home in a daze. This wasn't happening. This wasn't possible. Surely this was just some rebound mental lapse of reason.

I got home and plonked my new gym clothes on the dining table when I saw the box of the things Graham left behind. I went to it and ran my fingers over the sweater folded and shoved on top. I didn't know what anything between Reed and me meant. I didn't know what I wanted. I didn't know what I was capable of right now. But I knew one thing for certain. I picked up the box and put it outside by the front door. I'd take it up to Vinnies Charity Shop tomorrow.

That part of my life was over. Who I was when I was with him was gone.

With a satisfied smile, I went back inside and cooked dinner.

———

ANIKA AND SEAN arrived around half five, and by then I had entrées of grilled prawns with a honey and chili sauce, a main course of pork tenderloin and salad, and dessert of glazed fig and pear with honeycomb wafers and yoghurt.

"Sweet mother of God, this smells so good," Anika said as she walked in to my kitchen. She and Sean inspected all the food, then she kissed my cheek. "I love it when you get in a cooking mood."

"Jesus," Sean said. He looked at Anika. "Why can't you cook like this?"

"Same reason you can't," she quipped back at him. "You burn toast."

Sean rolled his eyes. "One time! I burned toast one time." He smiled at me then produced a bottle of wine. "It's not schnapps."

"Thank God," Anika mumbled.

I agreed. "Never again."

"I saw the box by the front door," Anika said softly.

I nodded. "Getting it out of the house felt right. We don't need to burn it. There's a charity shop up on Darling Street. I'll take it up there in a day or so."

She smiled at me. "Good for you."

"You look good, Henry," Sean said. "I haven't seen you in a few weeks. You can really see a difference. How much weight have you lost?"

"I don't know. Reed said it's best not to get caught up on numbers. He said I should see a difference in my clothes and fitness levels before the scales change."

Sean nodded. "Well, I can definitely see a difference. You've lost a few inches for sure."

"Definitely." Anika hummed. "So, Reed, huh?"

Instead of answering, I picked up a plate of grilled prawns and handed it to her. "Take it to the table please."

I knew Anika was itching to ask me what happened today, what warranted my call to her after I left his house sounding a little freaked out. But we at least managed to get through dinner first. Sean planted himself in front of the Sunday football, and Anika and I sat at the table, our empty plates and dishes pushed away. "I'll clean it all up later," I told her.

She didn't argue. She just poured me a small glass of wine and sighed. "How are you doing, Henry?"

"I'm okay." It wasn't a lie. It just wasn't the whole truth.

"Are you lonely?"

I thought about that for a moment. "Not really. I thought I would be, but maybe Graham and I didn't talk as much as I thought we did. I can't really decide exactly what's changed since he left. I take both bins out now. I don't buy as much coffee. He did clean the bathroom and he'd do my laundry about as often as I did his. But I don't know. There's no gaping hole where he used to be." I sighed loudly. "I look around my house, now he's not here, and can't find anything different."

Anika put her hand on mine.

"Were we that bad?" I asked. "Were we so lifeless and mundane and I was just blind to it? Because I thought I was happy, but I'm pretty sure I was just comfortable. I was happy just knowing he was a constant thing, but we didn't have a relationship. We had a mutually agreeable companionship."

"Maybe," she said cautiously. "I think all long-term relationships are hard work, and complacency is a death sentence."

"True." I nodded and sipped my wine. "We had spark and we were vibrant and colourful in the beginning, but things had been monochrome for a long time. I can't explain it any other way. I don't remember there being one point where things changed. It wasn't bad, and we never fought. We just got complacent. I can see that now. I can see why Graham wanted out."

"And what about Reed?"

"I don't know."

"What don't you know?" Anika's brow furrowed. "Because I'll tell you what I know. You spend a lot of time together. Outside of the gym. You hang out together, you talk on the phone for over an hour. You smile more now than I can remember seeing for years. You look happier, Henry. And it's because of him."

"It's just flattering and good for the ego," I admitted. "Being dumped because I'm old and overweight wasn't exactly good for my self-esteem. But Reed tells me I'm doing great, and he says nice things to me, and it's pretty fucking sad that I need to hear it from some guy I'm paying to help me lose weight."

She frowned. "I tell you these things. You don't pay me."

"I pay you in food and wine, and daily phone calls."

"True." She sipped her wine and sighed. "But it's more than that with him, Henry. And you know it. You don't pay him to take you to the markets or to spend the day with you in the city. The phone calls, text messages, coffee at his place..." She looked at me sincerely. "I think he likes you, Henry."

I shook my head. "Not possible."

"Why not?"

"Have you seen him?"

"Actually no, I haven't. Looks don't matter, Henry."

"They do when you look like him. Guys hit on him all the time. Like today! God, I thought that sales guy was gonna drop to his knees in the change rooms."

"And what did Reed do?"

"He said he wasn't his type, so he pretended we were boyfriends so the other guy would leave him alone."

Anika raised an eyebrow at me.

"But it wasn't like that."

"And what did he do when he met Colin and James?"

"He pretended we were boyfriends so they'd think..." Anika pursed her lips, raising both eyebrows this time. "It wasn't like that."

I took out my phone and scrolled through Facebook until I found the gym's page and then showed her photos of Reed.

Anika's eyes widened. "Holy shit."

"See what I mean! He looks like Chris Hemsworth! Just better. God, even the buffed up guys at the gym hit on him all the time. And I'm pretty sure some of them are straight."

"And what does he do about it?"

"Nothing. He said they're not his type."

"He has a few not-types. What actually *is* his type?"

"I don't know."

"Maybe you should ask him."

I shook my head. "It's too soon. I don't want him to be some rebound guy because he's better than that."

"Because you like him more than you're admitting."

I drained my wine in one mouthful and glared at her. "Shut up. You're bad for my liver."

"So, you think you're not ready emotionally? Or is it something else?"

I'd been friends with Anika long enough to know there was no avoiding something if she wanted to get to the bottom of it. It's what made her great at her job and really fucking annoying as a best friend. "Both. I don't know. I'm not ready. I need to be me for a while."

"And?"

"And you've seen him?" I waved my hand at my phone. "He's so out of my league. It's not possible outside of those cheesy Hollywood movies."

Anika gasped. "You love those movies!"

"Not when it's reality. And the very likely reality is that Reed had a bet to see if he could make the fat gay boy cry like in *Can't Hardly Wait*." I felt bad for even saying that.

Anika gawped at me. "Do you think that's what he's doing?"

"No. I don't. He wouldn't do that."

"Then give him some credit. Though the scene at the end is excellent. You'd make the best prom queen."

I sighed. "I know, right?"

Sean laughed from the couch. "Sorry. Don't mind me."

I looked at Anika, and she took both my hands in hers. "What am I doing?" I whispered. "I thought I had my Mr Forever with Graham, but as it turns out, I spent the last six or so years deluding myself. You know what's worse than being alone?"

She squeezed my hands. "What's that?"

"Being with someone and being alone at the same time."

Anika frowned. "Oh, honey."

"I didn't realise how alone I was when Graham and I were together. Until he left and I actually was alone, and truthfully, nothing was different."

"And how does Reed make you feel?"

"Happy. But..." I added the all-important *but* before she could get carried away. "But would anyone else make me happy, or is it just him? What if I walked into another gym, or what if a different personal trainer took me on, would I like spending time with them too? Maybe it's just the attention and new conversations, the new direction that makes me happy. I don't know."

Anika seemed to consider that possibility. "I'm pretty sure no other personal trainers spend that much time with clients outside of work, Henry."

"What are you saying?"

"I'm saying, that if you happened to get a different personal trainer, they're not going to the markets with you, they're not spending Sunday afternoons in the city clothes shopping and inviting you back to their place for coffee. That's what I'm saying. I think Reed does that because he likes you."

"What do I do?"

"You like him, I know you do. You can't lie to me, Henry,

you've never been able to." Anika sat back in her chair. "You need to decide if you want to act on it? If you want to wait? If you're happy to just let it go? Only you can answer that, Henry."

"What would you do?"

She looked at me like I was crazy. "If that picture you showed me was Reed, I'd be climbing him like a freakin' tree."

"Hey!" Sean protested from the sofa. "I'm still here, you know!"

Anika gave him her puppy dog eyes. "I know, my love." Then she turned to me and whispered, "But Reed's really hot."

"Yep." Sean said, nodding slowly. "Still here. Still not deaf."

"Still not Chris Hemsworth," Anika replied. She took my phone and walked over to the back of the sofa, pulled Sean's head back, and planted a kiss on his lips. "But I'd climb you like a tree too." Then she showed him the photo of Reed at the gym that I'd shown her. "See?"

Sean took the phone and inspected the image. It was a photo of Reed in a muscle shirt lifting weights. It was a candid shot of him doing a workout, but he was sweaty and smiling. Sean let out a low whistle. "Yeah, okay. I'd probably climb him like a tree too."

I groaned. "You guys aren't helping."

Anika came back to join me at the table. She slid into her seat and handed me my phone. "But it's not just what he looks like," she said. "You're not a superficial person, Henry."

"Of course I'm not."

"But I have to know..." Anika bit her lip and waggled her eyebrows. "Is he in proportion?"

I swatted her hand. "I don't know. I haven't seen... that part of him." Then I remembered the one pair of jeans he tried on were tight enough that I could pretty much see that yes, he was in proportion. "Looks don't matter to me."

"If you say size doesn't matter, I'm gonna call you a liar liar, pants on fire."

I laughed at that. "Well, you've clearly never had anal sex with a man endowed with a horse dick."

Anika snorted. "Oh, I've had anal sex with a guy who has a huge dick. I just wasn't the one who bottomed."

Sean shoved his face into a cushion, mumbling something I couldn't make out, and Anika burst out laughing. She pointed to him and winked as she laughed. Then she pushed my shoulder and said, "Hey, why do you assume I'd bottom? Jesus, Henry, you know me better than that. I'm a top, through and through, honey. Please tell me you know Reed's a top, right?"

I had no doubt. And I could almost feel how good those calloused hands would scrape against my skin and how they'd feel as he manhandled me around the bed. "Oh yeah."

Anika nodded slowly. "You're picturing it right now, aren't you?"

"Shut up."

She clapped her hands together and stood up. "On that note, we'll be off."

Sean shot to his feet. "Yes. Because God knows, Henry doesn't need to hear more about our sex life. I'm really sorry about that."

"Don't apologise," I replied. "I like learning new things about my friends."

Sean rolled his eyes, and Anika kissed my cheek. "Love you, Henry. And for what it's worth, I think you should take a chance with Reed. And if it doesn't work out, then at least you get to have great sex with a guy with a horse dick."

Sean dragged her to the front door. "I'm considering

limiting your consumption of wine when you two are together."

They got half out the door when Anika tried to whisper and failed. "And I'm considering pegging you again when we get home."

Sean stopped, looked at Anika, then at me, then cleared his throat. Without a word, he turned and led Anika down the path. I closed the door with a smile and spent the next hour cleaning my kitchen.

I fell into bed, happy. Happy with the new direction, happy with the possibilities of what might be.

I didn't know if it included Reed. But I couldn't wait to find out.

NINE

MONDAY MORNING DRAGGED ITS SORRY SELF
through a tide of meetings, deadlines, and reports. The highlight was the morning tea, which Diana from Projections had
brought in for her contribution to the cook and share thing
that I had apparently started. She'd made some thin pastry-
type tart topped with roasted beetroot, feta cheese, and
balsamic glaze, which, according to her, she'd bastardised from
her grandmother's traditional Turkish recipe.

And oh my God. It was *so* good. I took a quick photo on
my phone, claiming it was so I could replicate the recipe later.

"You're sending it to Reed, aren't you?" Melinda asked.

I attached it to a message, hit send, and looked up from my
phone. "Of course."

She rolled her eyes. "How is it possible that you're losing
weight with all this food you do?"

Before I could answer, my phone beeped. It was Reed.

Looks good. When are you making that for me?

*When you make me that lamb salad you keep promising
but fail to deliver.*

Ouch. What about this Saturday?

Aren't you doing that trainer's challenge on Saturday?

Yes. In the afternoon. Last I heard, dinner is usually in the evening.

Ouch. Your place? Or mine?

Yours.

Melinda interrupted my texting. "If you keep smiling like that, people will think you're watching porn on your phone."

"I'm not smiling at my phone." I had to physically make myself pout so I wasn't smiling. "I'm doing lip stretches."

"Mmhm," Melinda deadpanned.

I leaned across our lunch table and whispered, "And who smiles when they're watching porn?"

"Happy people, and virgins."

I considered that and conceded with a nod. "Good point."

Melinda secured the lid on her lunch container and laid her fork precisely at twelve and six. "Don't forget your meeting at two with the boss," she said without missing a beat. "Any clue what that's about?"

I shook my head. "None. I assume it's the usual data analytics."

Melinda made a face that told me she didn't believe that. "If it were, then Lillian would've requested a statistics report."

"And she hasn't?"

Melinda shook her head. "No."

"Oh."

Melinda twisted her lips, and her eyes flashed with uncertainty. "Are we expecting corporate downsizing? Because the Melbourne office has."

Well, shit. "I hope not."

"You don't have to worry," she said quietly.

"And neither do you. Because we're a team, Melinda. I couldn't do this without you, and I'll tell them that."

In a rare moment of vulnerability, she gave me a timid smile. It was a far cry from her usual fierce and sarcastic self. "Thanks."

I reached over and gave her hand a squeeze. "I mean it."

As our lunch break drew to a close, Lena, Rihanti, and Kadin walked past our table toward the door. "Hi, Henry," Lena said. "How was your weekend? Do anything exciting?"

Oh God. Conversation. *Don't say something stupid, Henry.* "Good, thanks. Just the usual... drunk singing on tables on Friday night, and just so you know, schnapps has a lot to answer for. Spent all of Saturday dying because of schnapps. Again, not my fault, and Sunday was a mix of incredible and horrifying. So yeah, just the usual."

They all blinked in unison, and I mentally congratulated myself for not saying something too stupid. Melinda covered a laugh with a cough.

"Sounds fun," Rihanti said slowly.

"How was yours?" I asked. See? I could do conversation. I preened a little at my adulting skills.

"Quiet, by comparison to yours. Just family stuff, you know how that is."

I nodded, because yes, yes I did know.

"I hate schnapps," Kadin said. "Had a terrible experience with it back in university and haven't been able to drink it since."

"I can't do tequila," Lena offered, making a face. "Ever again."

I chuckled at that. "Oh, I remember this one time at university, my best friend and I got so drunk on ouzo we——" Then I remembered how that ended. "Never mind. That story isn't appropriate for work. Actually that story isn't appropriate at all, though I'm sure the police and Surry Hills Fire Department still talk about it."

Now they all stared at me, Melinda included. "Fire Department?" she asked.

"Oh, we didn't start a fire," I clarified. "It was more of a rescue..." I cleared my throat. "I was young and impressionable. That was a *long* time ago. You know, Anika really is a bad influence on me."

"Anika says the same thing about you," Melinda said, standing up. "Just be grateful it was pre-Internet days."

I stood up too and picked up my salad container. "Are you kidding? I'd be an Internet sensation. Apparently my schnapps-induced rendition of *Les Mis* on Friday night was worthy of Broadway."

Melinda fought a smile. "Did anyone get it on video?"

I blanched. "God, I hope not." I looked at the others then leaned in towards Melinda. "Do me a favour? Search YouTube for 'gay man singing "Drink With Me" on a table at the London Hotel,' and if you find any, send a takedown notice, effective immediately."

Again, they all stared at me, and I realised what I'd just said. *Gay man.* Fuck.

Like she could see the panic bubbling inside me, Melinda straightened her back. "Right, lunch is over. Back to work." She used her scary voice, and even though she was tiny, most people jumped when she spoke like it was possible she was vying for world domination in her spare time.

I didn't really notice where the others went, but Melinda led me to my office. When the doors closed behind me, I pointed to the now obscured hallway. "This is why I don't speak to people at work!"

"Henry, take a deep breath," Melinda ordered. She put her hands on my shoulders. "Everything's fine. I know it's scary, but I like that you're speaking to our colleagues more. They like you. I wish you could see that." She waited for me to exhale. "I'm pretty sure they already knew you were gay."

"What? How?"

She clicked her tongue. "Well, there was that time you told David from the mailroom that he shouldn't wear tweed with polyester."

"Because it's the truth," I whispered.

"I know it is." Melinda nodded sympathetically. "Then there was that time you gave colour palette lessons to Eliza from Admin because her lipstick was too fuchsia for her complexion. Remember?"

I nodded slowly. "I was just helping. But it reinforces why I shouldn't speak to the people I work with."

"No. It reinforces who you are. And they like you, Henry. You're good at your job, you're just a little direct. Because there was also that time when you told the national director that Idrina's report on the influence of globalization on China's economy was brilliant."

"Because it was."

"Idrina smiled for a week. And her report was then read and implemented on your recommendation."

"She deserved recognition for that."

Melinda smiled at me. "People like you, Henry. And they've known you were gay for years. Don't be afraid to show them the real you."

I sighed long and loud, trying to believe what she was saying, trying not to panic. "Do you think there is a YouTube video of me drunk and singing on a table from last Friday night and Lillian saw it? And that's why she wants to see me? Because I'm pretty sure a boss can fire me for that." I put my hand to my forehead. "Oh God, what if it's trending on Twitter?"

Melinda laughed. "No Henry. I'm sure there's no footage."

"Can you check?"

She channelled her inner Google-fu, typed in a bunch of

different keywords, and thirty seconds later said, "I can't find anything."

I sighed the mother of all sighs. "Thank God."

She checked the time. "Ooh, Henry, you need to go."

Crap. It was almost two. I combed my fingers through my hair and straightened my tie. "Look okay?"

"Perfect. Now go."

Meetings with Lillian Caldwell always made me nervous. She was a great boss and one of the most intelligent people I'd had the privilege of knowing. She had brains, common sense, used logic and reason, and wore Prada like it was designed for her. She also had eyes like a hawk and missed nothing, called a spade a spade, and had no tolerance for bullshit.

I liked her.

Her assistant buzzed me through and I made my way into her office, certain she could smell my curiosity and dread. She looked up from her desk and smiled. Okay, so smiling was good. "Come in, Henry. Take a seat."

I did as she said, sitting with my hands clasped on my lap, squeezing my fingertips nervously.

"Talk to me, Henry."

"About what?"

"I've been watching you these last few weeks."

Well, that was weird. "Oh?"

"With the exception of my time in Singapore and Melbourne, of course. Stepping up into this role isn't easy." She nodded slowly. "Though your analysis of the ACX reports was good."

Why was she bringing this up? "Was something amiss?"

"No, Henry, of course not."

I relaxed immediately. "Oh, I was worried there for a moment."

She smiled at me, keeping eye contact, and I realised this wasn't her professional face. *Was she about to dip her toe into personal waters?* My heart rate started to spike... I think I'd prefer to be fired. "In all your years here, you've been a closed book," she said coolly. "Nothing short of proficient, courteous, and impeccably professional."

Oh God. This wasn't going to be personal at all. This was sounding a lot like Graham's 'it's not me, it's you' speech... "Am I being fired?"

She blinked in surprise then laughed. "Good heavens, no Henry." Her smile softened, and she straightened the pen on her desk. "I wanted to talk to you today about some changes I've noticed. Something has changed for you in recent weeks, and I'm not the only one to notice it."

I swallowed hard. "I've had some changes in my personal life. I thought I kept a distinct line between work and home, but clearly not as good as I thought. I apologise if it's had a negative impact on my performance, and if any colleagues——"

Lillian put her hand up and stopped me. "Henry. It's quite the opposite actually. It's been noted you've been talking and laughing with a few people around the office, which is new. And I'm led to believe this new Monday morning tea that everyone's talking about was your idea."

"Oh. Well, accidentally, yes." Lillian waited for me to explain. "I brought in a citrus tart for Melinda, and she shared it with everyone, and so the idea was born. If it's a problem, I can tell everyone to stop. Though we have made a note of allergies and religious concerns to make sure it's safe for everyone."

Lillian smiled. "It's no problem. In fact, I think it's a great idea. It's been a great morale booster throughout our floor, and whether it was started accidentally or a planned initiative, Henry, you're to be congratulated."

"Oh. But it was really Melinda's idea..."

"And the change in your inter-office relationships? For six

years you've barely spoken freely with anyone, but now you are."

"Is that a bad thing?"

"No, not at all. Just a noted change. I walked past some people and overheard them saying how nice this change is in you. Is everything okay?" She seemed to sense my hesitancy. "You can speak freely with me, Henry."

"Yes, thank you. Everything's fine." I was going to leave it at that, but her imploring gaze made me panic. "I found myself suddenly single after eight years."

"Oh." She schooled her features quickly. "I'm sorry to hear that."

"I was too. But as it turns out, there have been some silver linings."

"Well, I'm glad, Henry. Did you need some personal time?"

"No, no. In fact, I feel like I've been more focused and have more energy for work than before." Then my filterless brain went on a possibly career-ending rampage without me. "See, I've started a new exercise program because my ex decided I was too old and fat for the life he wanted to live. Anyway, I have a personal trainer now and a new dietary plan. I work out three times a week, and I feel great. I didn't in the beginning, I thought I was going to die, but now I feel so much better. It doesn't hurt that my personal trainer is lovely and sexy as hell, even though he's making me do the Bay Run, which might possibly kill me, I'm kind of looking forward to the challenge."

Lillian stared at me, her expression unreadable.

"Okay, sorry, this is generally why I don't speak freely at work. When I first started here, Graham thought it would be best if I didn't engage in conversation, for reasons which are now clearly obvious."

"Graham?"

Oh crap. I cleared my throat. "Ah, yes. He would be my now ex-partner."

Lillian continued to eye me, and eventually she gave a small smile. "Henry, I was unaware you are gay."

And suddenly I felt stripped bare and very defensive. I swallowed hard and took a second to speak. "I trust it's not an issue."

Her eyes softened and she held up her hand. "Not at all. I'm just sorry you felt you couldn't tell me sooner." Then she tilted her head. "Is that the real reason you never attended any Christmas parties?"

"Mainly. That and my lack of ability to hold conversations without rambling like a socially inept unit, much like I am now. Add the possibility of alcohol at a Christmas party, and I'd be singing *Les Mis* on tables and giving people unsolicited fashion tips."

Lillian fought a smile. "I see."

I sighed. "I can talk about work, figures, statistics, and probabilities all day long. Give me reports and data files, and I use them like a shield. But talking freely about personal subjects has always been a concern. Sorry. I'm trying to do better, but I lack a filter, and after all these years of not engaging in conversation with anyone I work with, it's not an easy feat."

"Well, I'm glad you're trying. It's been a welcome change to see you smiling this last week or so. And I want in on the Monday morning tea thing."

"Well, I don't think there's any left. It was really good today."

She laughed. "No, I mean I want to cook something and bring it in."

"Oh! Yes, for sure! I think there's a list in the breakroom where you can add your name on which Monday suits you best. I think the others would love that."

Lillian smiled. "I'll do that. Oh, and just a heads up, I'll be away for two weeks next month, and I've listed you to be my replacement again. I know two weeks is the longest you've had to assume that responsibility, but I think you're up for it."

"Yes, of course! I'd love that." I couldn't help but smile. "Two weeks? Where are you off to this time? I wasn't aware of any scheduled conferences next month."

"No, this is personal leave."

"Oh. Sorry, I didn't mean to assume..."

"It's fine Henry. My partner, *Megan*"—she gave me a pointed stare—"insisted I take a vacation. So I'm taking her to Tahiti."

I almost laughed. She was a lesbian? I had no idea. But it explained her smooth reaction to finding out I was gay, and I understood very clearly this was not news she shared with many. I felt privileged and honoured that she'd shared it with me. "I hope you both have a lovely time. You deserve a break. You've worked nonstop for months."

"That was Megan's argument."

I stood up, and figuring hugging her was unprofessional and giving her a fistbump and saying 'gay power' wasn't strictly code either, I said, "Thank you, Lillian."

She gave me a warm smile. "Any time. If you ever need to talk, my door is always open. And Henry, I like that you're being more yourself now. There's been a few more smiles around the office lately, and that hasn't gone unnoticed."

I gave her a nod. "Thanks."

I went back to my office, still unsure to the underlying purpose of the meeting, and Melinda quickly closed the doors behind me. She looked around like a meerkat. "Well?"

"I don't really know what that meeting was about."

"What did she say?"

"Just that my now talking to people has been noticed, and

the Monday morning tea share thing is to be commended. I told her it was your idea, by the way."

"So no one is being made redundant?"

"No."

"She just wanted to chat with you?"

I nodded. "I told her I'm gay."

Melinda blinked, then blinked again. "Why?"

"Well, I just started talking, and you know how that usually ends for me. With the mindless babbling, uncensored drivel..."

She nodded knowingly. "And?"

"And nothing. She just wished I'd felt more comfortable to tell her earlier."

Melinda looked around my office like she was seeing it for the first time. "Wow."

"I know, right? And she's going on two weeks annual leave next month, and she wanted to know if I was comfortable in stepping up for that length of time."

"Henry, that's incredible!"

"It is," I agreed. This was better than any promotion I'd got. Normally those were a formal application with a formal approval, but this was an informal, personal chat with the boss. And not even the Australian Government Residual Interest Report in my in-tray, which meant I'd be here until late, could dampen my mood.

I STILL HAD a bounce in my step when I got to the gym the next morning. "Hey," Reed greeted me with his usual cheerful smile. "You're looking bright-eyed today."

"I am. And you're going to tell me there's no workout today, only coffee."

He grinned and waved a piece of paper in front of me.

"Actually, I have your new workout all done. You'll be ready for the Bay Run in two weeks."

"Two weeks?" My voice squeaked. "What happened to next month?"

"You're ready now," he stated. "You could do the Bay Run today."

"Sure I could. But I'd rather run it and then not die."

Reed laughed. "You're not going to die. And you're not even going to run it. Not the whole way, anyway. I have it in your new schedule here, jogging then walking, alternating for five kilometres."

"You mispronounced no workout only coffee. I'm pretty sure that's what you were going to say."

He just chuckled. "Come on. Treadmill time."

"I hate the treadmill."

"I thought you hated the elliptical."

"I hate them equally. I can't have one thinking it's the favourite."

I took out my water bottle and sweat towel and stepped up onto the treadmill while he programed something into it. "I can't be running 5Ks before work. I'll be hopeless at work all day."

Reed jumped up onto the treadmill next to mine and pressed a bunch of buttons. "No you won't. You'll be surprised, Henry."

"I'll be surprised if I don't die."

He laughed again, not taking me seriously at all. And I was serious. This was going to kill me.

"So..." Reed looked at me a little apprehensively. "Any particular reason for the good mood?"

"Just a good day at work yesterday."

His smile was immediate, as if he was relieved? "Oh, I thought Voldemort might've finally called you back."

"What? No, no. And even if he did," I said without doubt, "I wouldn't be interested."

Now he grinned and clapped his huge hand on my shoulder. "Good. You're better than he deserves." Then he hit the start button on his treadmill and told me to do the same. And we jogged and walked and jogged and walked for five kilometres side by side.

I didn't even die.

TEN

THE FEW DAYS THAT FOLLOWED WERE GREAT. I mowed through my in tray at work, chatted with people on my lunchbreak, and had several text conversations with Reed. It was absurd how excited I was for my Friday morning session at the gym, and if anyone had told me four weeks ago I'd be looking forward to exercise, I'd have busted something laughing.

Or maybe it wasn't so much the exercise as it was the personal trainer.

I couldn't deny that I liked Reed. He was everything I was not: confident, gorgeous, fit. Desirable.

But he was also lovely and charming and funny and intuitive and kind. He was the type of person who would help people when others weren't looking, not for any kind of financial gain, but because of the kind of person he was.

Was he being nice to me out of pity? I didn't think so. It wasn't like him to do that. Was he being nice to me because it was his job? Well, that I couldn't be sure of. He smiled at everyone like he smiled at me, didn't he? I didn't know who else he called or texted or shared recipes with or went shopping with.

As I walked into the gym, I had to wonder if my infatuation with him was real or purely for my own ego. It didn't hurt that he boosted my self-confidence or that he starred in my dream last night, naked and glorious, and demanding...

"Hey." Reed smiled as he walked over to me. He had obviously just finished with another client and said goodbye as they left. He then focused on me and rocked up on his toes. Jesus Christ, could he somehow tell I'd had a sex-dream that included him last night? How is that even possible? Why did he have to look at me like that, and why did I blush?

"Hey." I nodded, remembering every detail of what he did to me my dream. "You were great by the way."

He half laughed. "What?"

Fuck.

"Sorry, I mean you *look* great, by the way." I felt my cheeks redden further.

"Uh, thanks?" He was clearly a mix of confused and amused. "You too. Love the new gym clothes."

"Oh, thanks." I cleared my throat and decided to start the whole conversation over. "So, what torture routine are we doing today?"

"Yes, right," Reed said, looking around the gym. He clapped his hands together. "Today we're doing more running and some core strength."

"Excellent."

He started walking over to the treadmills. "That didn't even sound too sarcastic!"

"I know. I believe the conversion has begun."

He put his hand on the treadmill but stopped and stared at me. "The conversion?"

"Yes, the brainwashing conversion to the dark side. You know, of the gym people? Those who actually *like* exercise."

Reed's smile was slow spreading. "Ah, that conversion."

I nodded knowingly. "Scary, huh? First there was cardio, then dieting. Who knows where it will end."

He chuckled. "I'm really glad to hear that, Henry. You've done really well to get this far."

"Thanks to you."

He held my gaze for a while, then looked away with a bit of a laugh. He let out a breath and turned his focus back to his job. "Okay, so to get the blood pumping, we'll do a slow jog but with no stopping. This is about pace and consistency. You'll want to slow to a walk, but I want you to push through it and keep jogging, okay?"

I cringed. "I take back everything I said about liking this."

He smiled victoriously. "No you don't."

He was right, though. I wanted to stop. I wanted to slow it down and walk a while to give my lungs some reprieve. I worried my feet would trip on the conveyor belt.

"You got this, Henry," Reed said beside me. He wasn't jogging with me this time but standing next to the treadmill, watching my every move. "Just pick a spot on the far wall and stare at it, clear your mind, and let your body do its job."

And strangely enough, that helped. It did clear my mind, and without consciously thinking about it, my legs kept moving and my lungs kept pumping. I could feel the sweat roll down my back, and it was good to know I could push through my own limits. I wouldn't have thought it was possible, but here I was, jogging my heart out. Proof that I'd made a decision to get control of my life back, and it was working.

Reed reached over and pressed some buttons and the machine started to slow down so eventually I was walking. And puffing and panting, but I was also smiling. "I did it."

"You did. You just ran three kilometres, nonstop." He checked the treadmill screen. "In twenty five minutes, eleven seconds."

I took a few deep breaths. "Is that good?"

"Very good. For you, that's excellent."

"For me?" I stepped off the treadmill on unsteady legs and wiped my towel over my face. "How fast can you do it in?"

"Well, that's not important."

"Yes it is."

"It's not a race, Henry. The only person's time you need to beat is your own."

"So if it makes no difference, then tell me."

He smiled and shook his head. "Nope. Come on, weights time. I'll give you a few minutes break. Have a drink of water, and we'll be using the free weights today."

He left me alone for a minute, giving me time to get my breath back and to stew over what time he could run three kilometres in. By the time he came back, my lungs were no longer on fire and I was breathing normally. I had the twelve-kilo dumbbells set aside on the flat bench.

"Lie down with your back on the bench, feet flat on the floor," he said as he walked back over to me.

I'm pretty sure he said something similar to me in my dream last night…

He ran me through some lifting, me lying on my back on the flat bench doing chest flies and him on his knees at my side. "Keep your abs tight," he said, touching my stomach. "Keep your arms even. That's it, perfect. Can you feel that in your pecs and core?"

I could feel him touching me in every cell of my body. "Yeah."

Then I had to think horrible thoughts, because lying down on a bench in gym shorts with him this close and touching me wasn't great for modesty. A hard-on right now would be horrifying.

"Okay, do another rep," he demanded.

Concentrating on lifting the heavy weights and not dropping them on my face worked well for killing hard-ons, and by the time I'd done another ten, I was sure I had it all under control.

But then he made it worse. "Okay, now stand up for me. Next up is bent-over rows. Like this..."

He rested one hand and one knee on the flat bench and lifted the dumbbell from the floor to his side. Which was fine for him, albeit very nice to look at, but not so much for me. Because being in a bent-over position with him close by sent a warm rush of blood straight to my cock. I did as he did, with one hand and one knee resting on the flat bench, trying really hard not to imagine him standing behind me, my gym shorts pulled down just enough to give him access, and him taking me deep...

"You okay, Henry?"

Shit, shit, shit. I'd forgotten to keep lifting the dumbbell, and God knows if I'd mumbled anything out loud. I cleared my throat. "Yes. I'm super fine, just dandy."

Super fine, just dandy? What the fuck, Henry?

"Is that Mary Poppins?"

Weights forgotten, I stood up straight and looked around the gym. "Where?"

Reed burst out laughing. "Never mind." He took the weights from me, and it was then I noticed Emily, Reed's closest friend, standing over near some client by the rowing machines, but she was watching us——or Reed, more to the point——and she was smiling. Reed was suddenly beside me. "Okay, on the floor, Henry. Face down."

"I've had better come on lines," I said without thinking.

Reed just laughed. "I should hope so." I got down on the floor, as did Reed next to me. "Plank, thirty seconds on, ten seconds off, three rounds. And go."

"Ugh," I whined. "Planking is ridiculous." I had so much

more to say on that subject, but planking and holding conversations was something I couldn't do at the same time.

Reed apparently had no trouble. "So what have you got planned for tomorrow night?"

I could only shake my head, and when the thirty seconds was up, I flopped to the ground and groaned. "I can only talk when I'm not planking, so I have ten seconds to say that I have no plans for tomorrow evening, and I'd like to meet whomever invented planking and poke them in the eyes."

Reed chuckled. "Okay, that's ten. Up for another thirty."

I lifted myself off the ground to resume the hellish planking position. I was starting to tremble, and Reed was doing it so easy, he looked like he could be watching TV.

"So if you're not doing anything, I still need to make that lamb salad, and you now have to make me that Turkish tart with beetroot that you sent me the photo of, so I was thinking you might want to do that tomorrow night?"

Jesus that sounded a lot like he was asking me on a date.

"That's thirty seconds," he said, lowering himself to the floor.

I crumpled to the mat with an *oomph*, though now my inability to speak wasn't from exercise. "I um... I'm..."

He gave me a smile that was almost sad. "Okay, that's ten. Last thirty seconds." He lifted himself effortlessly into the plank position, and I had to reef myself up with every bit of strength I had left.

"It's not a date, Henry," he said coolly. I think he even shrugged. How can he shrug while he's planking? Is he even fucking human? "It's no different from any other time we've hung out together. It's a non-date. So it's okay if you don't want to. You can just say no."

I shook my head. "Can't. Talk."

He chuckled and inspected the floor between his elbows until the timer put me out of my misery. I collapsed onto the mat. My stomach muscles were trying to kill me. I mumbled into the floor, "I better have abs of steel by the time I get to work."

Reed laughed then leapt to his feet like a cat. I'm pretty sure he wasn't human. I rolled over onto my back, and he held out his hand to me. I took it, revelling in the warm, calloused feel of it, and he pulled me to my feet.

"Are you still gonna come watch the trainer's challenge tomorrow?" he asked, the invite for dinner afterwards seemingly forgotten.

"Yeah, of course," I answered. "How long will it go for? I mean, what time is our non-date?"

He smiled. "I can be at your house at six o'clock?"

"Perfect."

It was then we both realised he still had hold of my hand. "Oh," he said, quickly dropping it and taking a step backwards. "Great workout today, Henry. You'll do the Bay Run next weekend easy."

"Or I'll die trying."

"You won't die, I promise."

I was totally going to die. "Just so you know, if our non-date will be my last supper, this lamb salad you're making better be good."

He chuckled warmly but looked over at his next client who was waiting for him. "I should go. I'll see you tomorrow."

I checked the time. Jeez, time seemed to fly when I was with him, and if I didn't hurry, I would be late for work. "Crap. So should I."

I collected my gym bag, and on my way out, Emily was behind the reception counter. She and Reed seemed to have some silent eye conversation, then she smirked at me. "Bye. Henry."

"Are you doing the trainer's challenge tomorrow?" I asked her.

"Yep. Gotta show these boys how it's done."

"I'll see you here then."

Her eyes lit up. "Are you coming to watch?"

"Yeah. Reed asked me to, so..."

Her grin was wide and warm. "Excellent. I'll see you then."

God, were fit and healthy people always so damn happy and cheerful? "Bye."

I flew home, showered, and dressed for work. My suit pants were loose now, and I had to cinch them with a belt. I noticed the shirt button at my throat wasn't tight, and I could even fit a finger or two underneath my collar. My jacket slid on easily, and I could do my shoelaces up without having to reach over my stomach.

I jumped back in my car, feeling better——thinner——than I had in a long time. I knew traffic would be slow going into the city, and given I had about twenty minutes before I got to work, I waited for my phone to connect to Bluetooth and hit Anika's number before I'd reached the end of my street.

"Henry," she answered. "Let me guess: you're stuck in traffic and the man in the car beside you is picking his nose."

I snorted. "Not today. Well yes, I'm stuck in traffic but no one's nose picking. I'm running a little late."

She paused. "You sound happy. What happened?"

"Reed asked me out on a non-date."

"Eeeeeeeee," she squealed, making me laugh. "Wait. What's a non-date?"

"Dinner at my place tomorrow, but it's not technically a date."

"Oh, it's technically a date."

"No, it's not."

"Tell me everything he said."

I relayed the conversation, and I could tell she was smiling when she spoke. "Henry, I don't want you to freak out. But it's a date."

"It's just dinner. He specifically called it a non-date."

"He called it a non-date because he didn't want you to freak out, but he still wanted to have dinner with you. It's a date, Henry."

I was grinning. I couldn't help it. "Do you think so?"

"I know!"

"He held my hand."

"He what?"

"He helped me up off the floor and kept a hold of it for about ten seconds."

She squealed again, and it sounded like she was bouncing in her seat.

I laughed at her. "Please tell me you're not in your office."

"Nope. Driving to North Sydney. Boring monthly meeting with Legal at nine thirty." She sighed loudly. "Um Henry, what were you doing on the floor?"

"Dying."

"Right."

"I had a sex dream of him last night."

Her laughter burst through the phone. "Was he good?"

"Of course."

"And let me guess. Hung too, right?"

"Like a horse."

It sounded like she was doing that weird jumpy-clap thing in her seat. "Oh, Henry, I do love you."

"Love you too."

"We'll talk later. And I want all the details. All of them."

I clicked off the call and made my way to the office. As much as I loved my job, as much as I enjoyed having newfound conversations with my fellow co-workers, I just wanted it all to be over.

I was excited for the weekend. I hadn't looked forward to

something like this in a long time. Sure, I'd enjoyed weekends with Graham, but we rarely did anything together. The lustre had been lacking in our relationship for a long time. I could see that now. And it was strange that I no longer felt sad or hurt by Graham's decision to end it. I was hurt by his words, and I was hurt by the cruel way he thought me so undeserving of an adult conversation instead resorting to pointing out my weight and how I chose to live my life. A simple "this isn't working out" would've sufficed. Then again, maybe if he'd been gentle with me, I'd have clung to hope that he'd come back. Maybe he'd been deliberately harsh with me so I would know it was truly over.

Whatever his reasons, I was no longer sad. I was no longer devastated. I was no longer a hot, pining mess.

I was relieved.

I was me again, but not just the old me. A new, better me. A healthier me. Mentally and physically, I was in a better place. I still had a long way to go. I wasn't denying that. But just four weeks ago, I spent a Friday night scared to be alone. I was a crying mess, eating my emotions with a side of cheesecake.

This Friday night, I was cooking healthy food while dancing around my kitchen to *The Best of the Bee Gees*. I fell happily onto my sofa to watch *Game of Thrones*, wrote out my weekly menu plan and shopping list, had a delicious bubble bath, and went to bed with every intention of fantasising about Reed and the things he would do to me.

Sprawled from one corner of my bed to the other, sated and smiling, I slept like the dead.

Eleven

There was quite a crowd at the gym for the trainer's challenge, which I wasn't expecting. They were clearly all regular customers, each person fitter and more muscled than the next. I recognised a lot of faces, and even though they smiled at me, I got the feeling they saw straight through me.

After all week of feeling good, of thinking I'd made positive steps forward, here with all these super fit people I felt like a frump.

I was pretty much the biggest person there. Well, the least muscled, the least buff. They all wore singlet-style muscle shirts, and admittedly, they wore them well. I had spent the last four weeks being sheltered by Reed, doing one-on-one classes, and not really noticing those around me. They were all perfect specimens of health and fitness, and I may as well have been invisible. They were all wearing the best brands, like they stepped off the actual ads and walked through the doors.

It hit me like a tonne of bricks that I didn't fit in here. I wasn't like them. I wasn't good enough, and I had been kidding myself to think I even compared.

"Henry!" Reed said, spotting me through the crowd. He made his way over, and by the time he'd smiled and said hello to a dozen people as he weaved through them, he frowned. "Hey, what's wrong?"

"Nothing," I lied. I looked around the crowded gym. "There's a lot of people."

"Yeah, everyone comes to see who wins."

I nodded slowly. "So? You ready to teach them all a lesson?"

He grinned. "Hell yes. I'm pumped for this."

"Okay," Lachie called out, wheeling a whiteboard out of the office. It had a sheet of some sort draped over it. "Trainers to the front."

Reed grinned and rubbed his hands together, and giving me a quick nervous glance, he made his way back through the crowd.

He joined Emily and three other trainers to stand at the front. They turned and faced the crowd, and the cheering and clapping and jibes and taunts started, and I had to admit, it was kind of exciting.

Out of all the trainer's competing, Reed was definitely the tallest. But any one of them could be a poster child for CrossFit. The two women trainers were slighter in build, but still well-defined and incredibly strong, with muscles I could only dream of. The men, on the other hand, had bulging biceps and shoulders, trim waists, and strong thighs. They each wore their gym uniform, and they each wore it very, very well.

Though Reed was by far the hottest.

Lachie pulled the sheet off the whiteboard, and the room was silent for all of ten seconds while everyone read the challenge routine. It was mostly a bunch of acronyms and percentage numbers next to weights that I didn't really understand, but everyone around me let out cheers and "oooohs" while the five trainers out the front actually doing the challenge all groaned. Well, except for Reed. He clapped.

I was starting to question his sanity.

"Okay, we start in five minutes," Lachie said. "Get your equipment ready."

They set off to grab dumbbells and barbells and weights that seemed ridiculous, and each participant had their own space at the front. By the time they got their barbells set up and had everything ready, the crowd——myself included——were lined up along the length of the far wall. Lachie set the wall clock on zero to start, each trainer stood at the ready, and with a loud and excited, "Go!" the clock started.

They started with burpees, jumping over their barbell in between each one. Their push-ups were some well-rehearsed mix of one-handed, two-handed, and some side reach thing that I think was purely for showing off. Then they did sit-ups, but not the normal ones I could barely suffer through. No, these were with their feet off the ground, doing some crunch/climb thing that hurt my abs just watching.

Everyone was clapping and cheering their trainer on, and Reed had his group of supporters. I found myself cheering along; the excitement was hard not to get caught up in. Reed was in the lead with one other trainer, who I'd seen before, but only learned his name by what people were yelling. Seth had one full sleeve of tattoos and a wicked grin, and he and Reed were clearly trying to outdo each other.

When they'd completed the sit-ups, they each jumped to their feet and ran to the wall. They picked up a twenty-kilogram medicine ball and, facing the wall, proceeded to throw it up to where the wall met the ceiling, only to catch it in a squat. Then pushing up, they would throw the medicine ball again. Checking the whiteboard, I deduced these were called 'wall balls.' I also deduced that I wouldn't have been able to pick up a twenty-kilo medicine ball, let alone throw it that high and squat at the same time. I also deduced Reed had really fucking hot thighs that bulged as he squatted, and his back muscles tightened his shirt very nicely.

They did that ten times, then dropping the ball, they ran back to their dumbbells and proceeded to do shoulder presses, then some single arm snatches. Jesus Christ. Reed's dumbbells were twenty kilos each! They did some obscene number of those, then went back to do wall balls, then back to dumbbells, and alternated that whole routine five times.

By the fifth round, both Reed and Seth were sweating and flushed. Seth was groaning through each shoulder press, and even though his arms and shoulders had to be burning, Reed just smiled. His chest was heaving; his sweaty shirt clung beautifully to his frame.

And if it were somehow possible, he was even better looking.

They finished that round and went to their barbells. Reed rubbed some kind of chalk on his hands, spread his feet, and put his hands to the bar, getting a feel for it before he lifted whatever absurd weight was on it. But before he started, Reed stood up straight and pulled his shirt off. Everyone clapped and cheered, and there was even a few "things are getting serious" and even one "Reed wins" from the crowd.

All I could do was stare.

Fuck.

I'd seen him wear singlet tops, muscle shirts, and tight T-shirts, but nothing——*nothing*——prepared me for seeing him shirtless. Perfect was such an overused word, and it hardly did him justice.

Physically, he was better than perfect.

Personality-wise he was pretty damn close, and I had to wonder what his fatal flaw would be. The flaw that killed how perfect he was to me. There had to be something...

He lifted the bar in some kind of Olympic snatch, every

muscle straining, his nostrils flaring, and pure concentration on his face. He did that five times, then dropped it, only to walk over to the overhead bar and do chin-ups like they were the easiest thing in the world to do. He did five of those, then went back to doing more weight lifting, alternating for five rounds.

It was insane and an incredible feat of human strength and determination. Seth was close behind him, then Emily and the others, but Reed was the clear winner. When he let go of the chin-up bar for the final time, everyone clapped and cheered, but he simply walked back to his barbell and dropped to the floor. He sat, taking deep breaths, sweaty, exhausted and spent, and watched his friends get through the routine. He clapped as each of them finished, and he cheered the final guy through.

And as I watched him, doing what he clearly loved surrounded by people he called friends, I figured out what was his one and only fault.

Me.

It was me that was wrong here. And I realised, with a stab of hurt and foolishness, that I was kidding myself if I thought for one moment Reed could be interested in me.

As the five trainers all caught their breaths, they high-fived each other and gave each other hugs. Seeing them with their hands on him and him with his hands on them, with their perfect bodies, it only further cemented the realisation that I was well and truly out of my league here.

Lachie wrote finishing times on the board, and when Reed was announced as the winner and as the crowd gave him high-fives and shoulder claps, I stood back and let them swarm him. When we made eye contact, I gave him a smile and nod, but before he could get to me, I slipped out the front door.

I drove home, and when lying on the couch wasn't reclusive enough, I kicked off my shoes and climbed into bed. I wrapped my blankets around my head, and wallowing in self-pity and misery, I took my phone and sent Reed a text.

Well done on the trainer's challenge. You deserved to win it. Sorry I had to leave. Wasn't feeling well. Will have to cancel dinner. Sorry.

Ten minutes later my phone rang. It was Reed's number. I wanted to answer it. I wanted to talk to him, to hear his voice. I wanted to make him laugh, I wanted to touch him like the other people had touched him. I wanted to tell him how proud I was of him for winning today, and I wanted more than anything to have our non-date tonight.

But I'd had a sharp reality check today, and my heart was hurting, and my ego was in a dark corner somewhere, licking its wounds. I pulled the covers over my head and let the phone ring out, only to have it beep soon after.

It was a text from Reed.

Henry? You okay?

"No," I spoke out loud. I didn't reply to the text.

My phone beeped again a little while later.

Henry, I hope you're okay. I'm sorry you had to cancel dinner. Can we take a raincheck?

I didn't reply to that either, and some hours later, I was still cocooned in my bed covers when my phone beeped again.

I hope you'll come in for our 8am session tomorrow. If not, I'll understand.

I didn't reply to that either but added a soul full of guilt to my self-pity and misery, and with a heavy, heavy heart, I rolled over. Buried in my blankets, I fell asleep.

There's something to be said about falling asleep at five o'clock in the afternoon, because I was awake at three in the morning and had nothing but guilt and low self-esteem to keep me company.

I felt awful for leaving Reed like that. It didn't change my place in his world, but I still felt bad. I wondered if he celebrated with his trainer friends last night, and then I had to wonder how fitness trainers "celebrated." Did they sit around eating quinoa and drinking kale juice, talking about negative calories and telling fat people jokes?

I sighed. That wasn't fair, and I knew it. Reed wasn't like that. And from what I'd seen of the trainers, none of them were. It was purely my perspective, not of them, but of myself.

I glowered at the ceiling until my internal anger threw me out of bed. By six o'clock, I'd cleaned my bathroom, mopped the floors, scrubbed the kitchen, and rearranged my Tupperware drawer, finding matching lids and neatly stacking containers that I promised myself to keep that way forever, but I knew in my heart of hearts it'd be a plastic catastrophe again by Tuesday.

I was at the gym a few minutes early with frustrated energy to burn and an apology for Reed at the ready. He was going through some weights with the two women who were normally leaving as I got there. When he saw me, he looked a little surprised, and it took him a few seconds to force a smile. I knew then that I'd hurt him, and the weed of guilt in my chest sprouted a few more vines.

"Hi, Henry," Emily said from the reception counter. "Reed's running a bit late today."

"Oh."

"He won't be finished for another twenty minutes."

"That's fine. I can wait."

She frowned. "Everything okay?"

"Sure." I shrugged. I found myself staring at Reed, unable to make sense of what I was feeling. I wasn't supposed to feel like this. I wasn't supposed to be attracted to him, not to anyone so soon after Graham left me. "Just, you know. Not really."

Emily shot Reed a look then tidied some papers on the desk that didn't really need tidying. "I think someone else feels like that too. He's not himself today."

I swallowed hard and took a backward step to the doors. "Shit. I should probably go."

Emily was around the counter in the blink of an eye and had her hand on my arm. "No, don't leave." She nodded toward the reception area. "Can we chat?"

"Um..."

I guessed it was a rhetorical question because she led me to the chairs and made me sit down. Apparently we were chatting whether I wanted to or not.

"I want to tell you something about him," she said quietly. "He's a real, genuine person, Henry. He sees the good in everyone, like to the point where sometimes he's a little naïve. I can say that because he's my best friend, and I adore him. He is literally the nicest person I know. But he has trust issues for reasons that are not my place to say."

"Why are you telling me this?"

"Because I see how you are together. I see how you look at him, and more importantly——well, more importantly to me——I see how he looks at you."

My heart tripped over itself. "What?" I shook my head. That wasn't true. "He's like that with everyone."

"No, he's not. He's professional with all the members here, but with you..." She gave me a half smile. "What you see is what you get with him, Henry. He can't lie; he can't hide his emotions. And he has two types of smiles: one he gives to everyone else and the one he gives to you."

I tried to make sense of her words. "He just smiled at me all wrong."

Emily sighed. "I think yesterday confused him. You left and cancelled your dinner date."

"He called it a non-date."

"Because he didn't want to scare you off."

My gaze shot to hers.

She smiled at that. "He said he mentioned dinner and you panicked, so he called it a non-date instead."

I was so torn. Her words were perfect, but there was still that dark cloud hanging over me that I just couldn't shake. "I'm sorry I left yesterday." I swallowed hard, trying to think of how to phrase this right. "I didn't want to, but it's pretty obvious I don't belong... here or with him."

Emily recoiled, like I'd just offended her. Who knows, maybe I did. "Why would you say that?"

"Because it's the truth. He's perfect and has the whole Thor/Chris Hemsworth thing going on, and I'm the Hulk. Not in temperament of course, and I've never been exposed to radioactive material, well, not that I know of. And I'm obviously not green. I just meant I'm huge and not particularly good looking..." I let my words die away when I realised my mouth was in fifth gear and my brain was stuck in neutral.

Emily reached over and put her hand over mine and gave it a squeeze, just as Reed walked his clients to the door. He said goodbye to them, with that professional smile Emily had mentioned, and he balked when he saw us sitting in the corner talking. He seemed frozen, and he was, again, having some eyeball conversation with Emily.

She nodded for him to come over and stood up. She held out her hand to me, which was odd, but I took it anyway. When Reed was close enough, she took his hand and placed mine in his. "You two need to talk. Henry, tell him why you left yesterday. And Reed, you know what you need to tell him." She walked back to her reception counter. "You're welcome."

Reed's hand was warm and strong, and just the touch of it eased the ache in my chest a little. "Henry," he whispered.

I looked up at him. God, he took my breath away. "Hey."

"I didn't think you'd show."

"I'm sorry I left yesterday."

He looked over his shoulder, and Emily was now over by the treadmills with other customers, probably giving us some privacy. Still holding my hand, Reed led me into the office where the scales and charts were. He closed the door behind us and let out a deep breath. He dropped my hand and wiped his nervously on his gym shorts.

"Why *did* you leave yesterday?" he asked.

Okay then, straight to the point. I put my hand to my forehead. "I'm not very good at this."

"What did you tell Em just now?"

"That I left because I realised I don't belong here." My heart was hammering, but I somehow swallowed down my fear. "Because I don't belong with you."

He did a double take. "What?"

The bubble of laughter that escaped didn't exactly sound sane. "I know, crazy right? That I would even think that I possibly could belong with you. I don't know why I did. Well, actually, that's not true. I can tell you exactly. Because the attention was nice. Because the conversations and the texting was the closest thing to a relationship I'd had for years. Because it made me realise that what I had with Graham had died years ago, and you made me feel special. You made me feel wanted and fun, and that was something I hadn't felt in a long time." I took a deep breath. "And I left because I really fucking stupidly thought I had a chance with you, until I saw you yesterday. Doing your trainer's challenge and being all superhuman and with all those fit and beautiful people, because I'm not like them. I'm a fucking blimp compared to them, and it was never more apparent than it was yesterday. You know, the *Sesame Street* thing where it shows four things and they all sing 'one of these things is not like the others'? Well, Reed, I am that one thing."

Reed was still staring at me, half horrified, half amused.

I shrugged, defeated. God, I felt like I'd just done a two-hour work out session. "I would still like to continue with my program, if that's okay. But I'll understand if you don't want to be my personal trainer anymore. I would miss our conversations and our recipe swaps, but I'm sure I'll get over it."

"I don't want you to get over it."

"Oh, okay, thanks. I can suffer for all eternity if you'd prefer."

He laughed, despite the tension between us. "No. I meant I don't want you to get over it, because I don't want it to stop. Our conversations and our recipe swaps, that is. And me being your personal trainer."

"Oh. Okay, good."

"But Henry?"

"Yes?"

"You do belong here. Just like any of the people who walk through those front doors."

He seemed to be missing the entire point of my whole tirade where I'd just told him I wanted to be with him, yet somehow ending with a song from my childhood. God, I hated my brain sometimes. "Was the *Sesame Street* song too much?"

"No. It was good. Perfect, actually."

"Perfect might be a strong word..."

"Henry, why don't you think you belong with me?"

"Oh." I blinked and stammered, "Um, well, God, it's just, um..."

"Do we not get on well?"

"We do."

"Do we not talk for hours and enjoy each other's company?"

"We do. Well, I do. Enjoy your company that is."

"I enjoy yours too." He waited and waited for me to answer his original question.

"I don't belong with you because you need to be with someone who looks like Seth."

"Like Seth?"

"Well, yeah."

"He's a nice guy, Henry. But he's straight and married with two kids."

"Oh."

"Do you think I need to be with someone because of how they look?"

"No!"

"Then what's the problem?"

"Because I've seen those movies where the hot jock acts all interested in the overweight nerdy person as a joke or a dare, and quite frankly, they're not funny."

He recoiled like my words physically hurt him. He took a step back then went from shocked to a little peeved. "Have I ever treated you any different?" He raised his eyebrows and folded his arms. "Have I ever once made you feel any less of a person?"

I put my hand up like it could somehow pull back my words that upset him. "No."

Reed's nostrils flared. "Because I'm insulted that you think that low of me."

I shook my head. "No, Reed, that's not what I meant. I would never think that of you."

"But you just did."

Oh Jesus, he was pissed at me. My mouth was suddenly dry. "Not just looks, no. I just thought you'd pick someone with a similar lifestyle. Not looks. Someone who respects their body and who spends time, hours actually, working out and being you know, capable of doing all those superhuman things you did yesterday."

He thought about that for a moment then shook his head. "I appreciate your concern for what you think I need. But how about you let me decide what I need and what I don't."

"Okay, yeah, that was presumptuous, sorry."

He nodded slowly. "It was. You seemed to have presumed a lot about me."

"I haven't really. Well, I haven't meant to."

"Is it about me, or is it about you?"

"What?"

"The one of us that's not good enough?" He frowned. "Is it me or you?"

"Me. God, me. You're——" I waved my hand in his general direction. "——you're perfect."

He shook his head a little and sighed. "It's hard to be pissed at you, Henry."

"No, it's not. A lot of people manage just fine."

He almost smiled. "No, I mean, it's hard to be mad at you for assuming all these crazy things when they all reflect your perception of yourself."

"What?"

"You don't think we should be together, not because I look like this." He waved his hand in front of himself like I'd done. "Because I'm, what did you call me?"

"Perfect."

Reed rolled his eyes. "Which is ridiculous, just so you know. No, Henry, you don't think we should be together because you don't think *you're* good enough."

I stared at him. I was ripped open, my heart and worst insecurities were exposed.

His eyes softened. "But, Henry, you are. And if you'd just

have asked me instead of shutting me out, I would've said that we do belong together. Because you get me, and I can talk to you and be with you like it's the easiest thing in the world."

I blinked and couldn't form the words. Coherent sentences were impossible. "Huh?"

Reed's lips twitched, and he finally gave in and smiled. He closed the distance between us until he stood close enough that I could feel the heat coming off his body. He put his fingers to my chin until I was looking up at him. I'd never felt more vulnerable than I did in that moment. My heart beat triple-time and my lungs squeezed, adrenaline and nerves flooded my body. He was so close and so tall, his size was over-whelming and incredible. His face was barely an inch from mine, his eyes an ocean of heat. He licked his lips and slid his hand along my jaw. The roughness of his skin sent a shiver through me, and he smiled.

"I'm going to kiss you," he whispered gruffly. "Is that okay?"

I couldn't speak, my throat was filled with butterflies, my brain was on an anticipation-high. All I could manage was a nod, and that was all the permission he needed. Reed tilted my head further back, and in a world-stopping moment, he slowly pressed his lips to mine.

His lips were warm and soft, and without words, he encouraged me to open for him. He deepened his kiss and slid his tongue against mine. The strangled moan he gave almost buckled my knees.

His hand around my jaw kept my mouth right where he wanted it and his strong arm wrapped around my back. He pulled me against him and he owned me with that kiss. I felt like I was floating, and then his tongue met mine again, and I thought I might catch fire.

I slid my hand through his hair, and it earned me a grunt,

and holy shit, the sound urged me on. This kiss was quickly becoming something else, and it didn't matter where we were, I wanted it.

The office door flew open, and Reed and I broke apart. Emily stood in the doorway, her surprise quickly becoming a grin. "Oh, sorry! I thought you guys had left."

Reed let out a nervous laugh and, standing half side on to her, protectively pulled me behind him. "No, we uh, didn't leave."

I peeked around Reed's arm. Emily was blushing a little, but her smile was genuine. "Carry on." She went to shut the door but stopped. "Actually, I was going to cover your last appointment anyway, if you'd prefer to... take this somewhere else?"

"We probably should," Reed said. "You're right."

"You can't miss your work for me," I said, looking up at him.

Reed turned to face me, confusion on his face just as Emily cleared her throat. "Just let me know. You've got about twenty minutes," she said, closing the door.

I put my hand on his arm. "Your next client will be expecting you."

"But what about this...?" He motioned between us.

"Oh, we can make out all afternoon."

He laughed. "I meant the talking."

"We can do that too." I took in his handsome face and his kiss swollen lips. "It's only an hour right?"

He nodded, and staring at my lips, he leaned in and kissed me again. Before we could deepen the kiss, he pulled away and took a step back. He let out a steady breath. "God, I can't go out there like this."

"Like what?"

He palmed his dick. His rather prominently hard, and noticeably large, dick.

"Oh." God, I could imagine how that would feel inside me. "*Oh.*"

He took a huge step back. "Not helping, Henry."

"Oh, I could help with that if you wanted me to."

He glanced at the door like he was weighing up his options, but then shook his head. "No, no. Our first time isn't going to be here."

"Oh, I didn't mean fuck," I whispered the last word. "I just meant I could——"

He squeezed his dick. "Ah, yes, I know what you meant. I meant our first time doing anything isn't going to be here." Apparently I couldn't hide my disappointment, because he laughed and pulled me in for a quick hug. "One hour. It's just one hour."

I mumbled into his chest, "Just think horrible thoughts."

"Well, I'm trying to, but all I keep thinking about is how you kiss, and that's not working at all."

I hummed. "God, you smell good."

He pushed me out to arm's length. "Okay, that's *really* not helping."

I took a step away from him, catching sight of myself in the mirror. I quickly looked away from my reflection and made a face. Something Reed didn't miss. He walked around to the filing cabinet and said, "Can I show you something?"

"If it will help with your rather large problem."

He stopped. "My what?"

"Your um..." I gave a pointed nod to the still-visible ridge line of his cock in his gym shorts. "That rather large problem."

Reed barked out a laugh, and the tips of his ears turned pink. "Oh." He readjusted himself and turned back to the filing cabinet. He pulled out a file in particular and slid it across the table. "Open that."

I doubted he'd be showing me anything I shouldn't be

seeing, so I turned the file around the right way. That was when I noticed the name on it.

Henry Beckett.

Me.

This was my file. I glanced up at Reed, and he smiled encouragingly. "Open it."

With a nervous breath, I flipped the folder open and saw my photo and a bunch of numbers on a chart on the first page.

"What's that?"

"Oh, that's just what I write down after every session. It shows your progress."

"Oh."

"Come over here," Reed said, picking up the folder and walking around the table to the mirror. "Stand in front of the mirror for me."

I wasn't comfortable doing this. At all. I didn't like my reflection a great deal. But I did as he asked, even if I didn't really look at myself.

"Look at this photo," Reed said.

It was the picture he'd taken the first day I came here. It was the image of the man who had cried in front of the bathroom mirror because he didn't like what he saw... I didn't like the photograph either.

"Now look at yourself in the mirror." He waited for me to do as he asked. "See the difference?"

And I could. I'd seen my reflection in the bathroom mirror every day for the last four weeks and never truly noticed a great difference. But here it was, right in front of me. My before photograph and me today.

The photo was me four weeks ago. I looked pale, exhausted, and sick, if I was being honest. Admittedly, it hadn't been a good few days, but I was also a lot bigger than I remember being.

My reflection today had clearer skin, with a healthier glow. There were no black circles under my eyes, and there was less weight around the neck and jaw and less weight around my middle.

"See the difference, Henry?"

I nodded. I could see the difference. Like holy shit, I could see a visible difference in just four weeks. It wasn't hugely drastic, but it was there. "Yeah." I smiled. "I can."

Reed beamed a smile at me. "Good. So next time you catch yourself in the mirror, please don't frown."

There was a knock at the door, then Emily stuck her head in. "Reed? Nadia's here."

"Yes, I'll take the appointment, thanks. I'll be out in a bit." Reed took the file and slipped it back into the filing cabinet. He walked right up to me and put both hands on my shoulders. He leaned down and kissed me softly. "Can you be at my place in about an hour and a half? There's something else I want to show you."

I nodded. "Sure."

He left to take his next client, and Emily smirked at him on the way out. When he was gone, she smiled at me. "Well, that went well."

I bit my lip so I didn't grin like a clown. "It did," I said. Emily looked around then stepped inside and closed the door, leaving just her and I in the room. Oh crap. "Is this the 'break his heart and I'll break your face' speech?" I asked, trying for jest, but I'm pretty sure she could smell my fear.

Emily laughed. "Not quite. I'm glad you two sorted it out. I want to see him happy, and I think he's had a thing for you since your first day. You made him laugh, and it's been a while since I've seen him smile like he does when he's with you." She studied her running shoes for a moment, then she looked right at me. "Please don't hurt him. His last boyfriend burned him pretty bad, and Reed might be a big strong guy, but that doesn't mean he doesn't get hurt."

I shook my head. "I wouldn't ever do that to him. I don't exactly know yet what Reed and I have, and to be honest, I still can't get my head around the fact he's even slightly interested in me that way."

Her lips twisted in a knowing smile. "He sees the person inside, Henry. And what you seem to think he should find attractive, isn't what he's after. He's one of those rare types that's attracted to things like honesty and humour."

"Oh. Well, those I have in spades."

"Believe it or not, he was worried about being good enough for you."

My eyes bugged out. "What?"

She laughed at my reaction, but there was a depth to her gaze. "I know, ridiculous right?"

"Why on earth would he think that?"

"Because you're corporate. You have a nice car, own your own house, and you're pretty good at your job in finance, or that's what he told me." Emily leaned against the wall and crossed her arms. "And he thought what he does for a living might not be good enough. You know, that you might not like telling people what he does for a job."

"That's absurd." I shook my head. "He loves his job. Do you know what half the people I know would give to be able to say that? And between you and me, I don't care what other people think. He could clean septic tanks and I wouldn't care." I made a face. "Okay, if he did that for a living, I'd probably insist he showered after work, but I wouldn't care what other people thought about it."

She finally gave me a smile. "Good."

"I thought this wasn't going to be a 'break his heart and I'll break your face' talk."

Emily shrugged. "Well, maybe just a little bit."

I couldn't help but laugh. "It's fine, really. I don't mind. I'm pretty sure Anika will give Reed the same spiel. She is to me what you are to him, and you two would get on like a house on fire. But I think we're getting ahead of ourselves. Reed and I still really haven't talked about, well, anything yet."

"Yeah, I know. Sorry. Just getting in early. You're going to his place after here?"

I nodded. "He said he has something to show me."

Emily gave me a genuine smile. "Good."

"You know what it is?"

"I'm not saying anything. Just be gentle with him. And honest. That's all I ask."

Okaaaaay. My interest was piqued. "I should go. He's probably wondering what the hell we're talking about in here."

Emily opened the door and Reed, who was helping Nadia with weights, shot a look in our direction. He was definitely wondering what we were talking about. He glared at Emily in a 'what did you say to him?' kind of way, then looked at me with sorry in his eyes. I gave him a smile to let him know we were all good, and Emily simply raised her chin unapologetically.

Yep. She and Anika would get on well.

Speaking of Anika, I knew I owed her a phone call. I gave Reed an awkward wave as I left, and I got into my car and called Anika on the drive home.

She answered her phone with, "The reason I'm only hearing from you now better have involved the best sex you've ever had."

I snorted, thankful no one else was in the car with me. "Not exactly."

I relayed the events of the last day, including Reed winning the superhuman challenge with his colleagues, then my freak out and subsequent cocooning in my misery and blankets, and what happened this morning.

"He kissed you?"

"Oh boy, did he ever. I have *never* been kissed like that."

She laughed. "What do you think he's showing you?"

"I have no idea."

"Do you think it could be a rubber doll collection?"

I burst out laughing. "Well, I'm pretty sure it's not."

"What if it's some weird fetish, like he has a thing for shoving live fish up his arse?"

"Jesus Anika, have you been watching *Bizarre Fetishes* again?"

"Maybe."

Dear God, she made me laugh. "I'm sure it's nothing like that."

"You mean, you hope it's not. Unless you actually like that kind of thing, in which case I can start calling you Fish Sticks."

"I'm going now."

"Would you use tartare sauce as lube?"

"Bye."

"Call me ASAP, okay?"

I ended the call and got out of my car, going inside to get changed. Only this time when I was getting dressed, I took the time to look at myself in the mirror. I still wasn't too comfortable with my appearance, but Reed was right. I could see the changes. Not just to my body, but in my confidence as well. I was a long way from where I needed to be, but I could see all my hard work was paying off.

I pulled on some jeans I hadn't been able to wear in years. I checked my arse in the mirror from a few different angles and had to admit, it didn't look too bad. My stomach was noticeably smaller and the T-shirt I pulled on was flattering my body instead of hiding my biggest flaws.

I stared at myself in the reflection for a while, and instead of shrugging off a 'it'll have to do' mentality, I was kinda happy with how I looked.

I wasn't perfect. In fact, I was far from it. But I was taking control of my body, of my mental headspace, and of my life.

With a nod to myself in the mirror, I went to Reed's place. I wanted to know what it was he had to show me, and I really wanted him to kiss me like that again.

TWELVE

REED OPENED HIS APARTMENT DOOR, FRESHLY showered, wearing his new jeans and plain grey T-shirt that seemed to defy the laws of stretch and comfort. He grinned when he saw me, and he stepped aside. "Please, come in."

He smelled of soap and deodorant, and suddenly my nerves kicked in. Or was it anticipation? The butterflies in my stomach couldn't tell the difference. But then I noticed him, or rather, noticed how nervous he was.

He licked his lips and wiped his hands on his thighs, then ran his hand across his stomach like he was in knots inside.

I went to him and put my hand on his arm. "Hey. You okay?"

He let out a breathy laugh. "Yeah. Bit nervous."

A bit? "Don't be. It's just me."

He gave me that eye-crinkling smile and let out a deep breath. "It's been a weird few days, huh?"

"Well, the weirdness yesterday was all mine. I freaked out, and I'm sorry. But this morning was great, actually." I blushed as I remembered the way he kissed me, and the memory of what his mouth could do made me warm all over. "You can kiss me like that anytime."

He barked out a laugh. "Ah, yeah. About that... I should apologise for how my body reacted to that." His cheeks tinted pink. "That was embarrassing."

I trailed my hand up his arm, feeling the swell of his biceps and the heat of his body. My eyes met his, and I whispered, "Don't apologise for that."

Reed took a step back and let out a shaky breath. "Okay, wow." He laughed and shook his head, as if to clear it. "I need to tell you something first. I want to kiss you again, but I want to be honest with you before we decide what we're doing."

Okay now I was officially worried. Anika's conversation came back to me. "Does it involve fish in any way?"

"What?"

"Never mind."

He chuckled, and taking my hand, he led me to the kitchen. Okay, the kitchen was a weird place for this conversation and not what I expected, but I went along with it. He left me leaning against the kitchen counter, then putting a distance between us, he leant against the opposite counter. He fidgeted with his hands until deciding to shove them in his pockets. "Em told me what you and her talked about."

I nodded. "Yep. She gave me the shake down. She didn't threaten me exactly, but we all know she could snap me in half, so it didn't really need saying."

Reed smiled. "She's just worried about me. That's all."

"I'm glad she is."

"Me too." He took a deep breath. "I was kinda down yesterday afternoon. After you disappeared, I thought for sure I wouldn't see you again. I have to admit, I was surprised to see you this morning."

"I needed to apologise. I really am sorry for leaving yesterday. I had hoped something was building between us, and then when I saw you without your shirt on, being all fit and gorgeous with other fit and gorgeous people, I let my insecurities win. And I'm sorry."

"Because you thought I couldn't possibly be interested in you..."

I nodded. "Yeah." I took a fortifying breath. If we stood any chance, I needed to be able to tell him this. "I mean, you could have any guy you wanted. And I'm... well, I'm not like them."

"Exactly. You're nothing like them. That's why. I wasn't joking when I told you I like that we talk about food and everything else. All the other guys I meet just wanna talk about lifting weights, protein powders, and how good they look. But you talk to me about real stuff. You make me laugh."

"But I'm... and you're..."

He folded his arms. "What?"

"Well," I tried to think of an appropriate comparison. "You're the Disney prince, and I'm Shrek."

He chuckled. "But you're not, Henry. And anyway, I happen to like Shrek." He let out a long breath, and his smile faded away. "Can I ask you something?"

"Sure."

"If I looked different, would this have been an issue for you?"

"What?"

"If I was big. If I was overweight. If I didn't look like this." He waved his hand in front of himself. "Would you have believed I could possibly be interested in you?"

I shrugged. "I haven't thought of that. I don't know. It would probably make more sense."

"You said this morning you thought I should be with someone who has a body type like mine——"

"No, I meant physical interests, like fitness and exercise. I'm sorry if that came out wrong."

He considered that apology. "So, if for example Anika was a plus-sized woman, would you tell her not to date an athletic guy?"

"No. Never. She's the best, if not craziest person I know. Someone, anyone, would be lucky to have her." There was more to this than he was letting on. "Why?"

"I'm trying to figure out what you really think about body image."

I shook my head, not sure why he was asking. "Okay, honestly? I hate it. I hate that people are given labels. Believe me, I've had enough labels to last a lifetime: gay, queen, fat, old. I wish the media would stop pushing unrealistic body images that cause kids to starve themselves so a company can sell a pair of fucking shorts. I wish bigger people weren't ridiculed and shamed and ignored. I wish people weren't judged for how they looked…"

And that stopped me.

Because that's exactly what I'd done. I'd judged him and his friends. I'd assumed so much about them, based purely on their physical appearances.

"Oh God." I put my head in my hands as realisation crept over me like a cold blanket. "I did that, didn't I? I'm sorry." Big warm hands were on mine, peeling them from my face. Reed lifted my chin, and I had to look up to see into his eyes. "I'm so sorry."

He leaned down and pressed his lips to mine. It was soft and sweet, and all too brief. He pulled back and almost smiled. "Thank you."

"I'm sorry for being a judgmental jerk."

He smiled kindly. "I want to show you something."

Oh, I'd almost forgotten about that. But I now understood why he brought me into the kitchen. Because there were photos on his fridge, and without another word, Reed pointed to one in particular.

It was a candid shot of a big guy. He was really tall, had a big belly, double chin. Young but very overweight, with familiar eyes. "Is that...?"

"Yes, that's me."

My gaze shot to his for a disbelieving moment, then I looked back at the photo. It really was him. The smile was the same, the eyes... My God.

"I was always the big kid." Reed smiled sadly. "You want labels? I had plenty. Chubby, lard-arse, fatso. When I was sixteen, I played football, front row. I crushed hard on the captain of the water polo team. He was gay, and as far as I knew, we were the only two gay guys in my year at school. We got on well, laughed together, hung out in the same crowd... Anyway, there was this party and we hooked up, but he said we couldn't be any more than physical. Like, he would never be my boyfriend because I was so fat."

"Did he say that?"

"He made it pretty clear."

"Oh Reed, I'm really sorry."

"That's why what Graham said to you really hit home for me. I know exactly what you felt like. I mean, I didn't have eight years with him..."

"But you loved him."

He nodded.

"What was his name?"

"Taj."

"Sounds like a captain of a water polo team. Suppose he was gorgeous and a total jerk."

Reed smiled. "Yeah. But can you see now? I would never judge a person by their body type because I've been there. I've been that guy for years that was called names and stereotyped, or worse, ignored, because he was big. I have been where you are."

I blinked back tears.

"But Henry, I am still the same guy that's in that photo. I am the same person now as I was when I was at my heaviest, yet people treated me differently. They treated me like I was a nobody, the butt of jokes because of my size. I mean, being six foot three at sixteen wasn't easy, and I was big. Like *really* big." He smiled with a far off look in his eyes as he obviously remembered something. "After Taj dumped me, I worked my arse off for twelve months: dieted, exercised, and I treated it like my job. Then I ran into him when we were eighteen, at a bar. He went off to college, and I hadn't seen him in, jeez, well over a year. He didn't recognise me at first, but he sure was interested. Then I told him it was me, and after he'd almost fallen over, I told him to fuck off."

"Good for you."

"And you look at me now and think I have it easy, but Henry, it's not. Because now the opposite happens. People only notice me for my body. They only want to be with me because I work out. It's all about weights and reps, and I love my job, but no one asks about *me*." He took a deep breath and licked his lips. "Until you. You wanted to know the real me." Then he put his hand on the photograph stuck to his fridge. "Because this is who I am. I'm the guy who knows what it's like not to feel good enough because of my body. And that's why it hurt when you assumed that of me."

I put my hand on his chest, over his heart, and looked up at him. "I'm sorry. I'm sorry I was a jerk."

Reed laughed. "You only said it because of your own insecurities, and that's something I understand. I've been there, Henry."

"I'm still sorry. I didn't realise how the stigma goes both ways."

He put his hand on my shoulder; his thumb traced my jaw. "So, now you know the real me, are you still interested?"

"Of course I am. More interested, I think. Thank you for showing me this part of you."

He took my face in his huge hands, and tilting my head back, he kissed me. Like really fucking kissed me. He owned that kiss, and in that moment, he owned me. I had never been man-handled before, by someone bigger and stronger, by someone who totally dominated me, and I had to admit it. I really fucking liked it.

I melted into him and let him kiss me however he wanted. He was all strong arms and sure hands, sweet lips and sultry tongue.

He pushed me against the kitchen counter, and he moaned as our bodies met. He snaked one of his arms around my back, holding me close to him, and he ran his other hand down over my hip, grinding us together. He broke our kiss to groan at the contact, then crushed his mouth back over mine, kissing me like he owned me.

I'm pretty sure I died right there. Or saw the light of heaven. Or was transported to some ethereal plane where pleasure and ecstasy were as tangible as air.

Reed broke away, with one hand on my hip, his other hand fisted in my shirt. He was out of breath and looked a little drunk. "Jesus."

I drifted back to earth like a feather. "Yeah."

"Just give me a minute," he said with a breathy laugh. "God, you do this to me."

I gripped my own hard-on. "Uh, I'm pretty sure it's you."

He looked at the bulge in my jeans. "Henry," he half growled, half laughed. "You're not helping."

"Oh, but I can," I said, taking his hand, leading him out of the kitchen. "Where's your bedroom?"

He pulled me to a stop. I looked up at him, wondering if I was moving too quickly. He put his hand to my face. "Are you sure, Henry?"

I met his darkened gaze. "Not full-on sex. I mean I want to, like really fucking want to, but I think it's too soon. We can take the edge off, yes?"

His nostrils flared, and he grabbed my hand and led the way. The midday sun lit his room and a soft breeze ruffled the curtains. His bed was king-sized, the covers were white and looked like clouds. He walked me into his room, and when the backs of my knees hit the bedframe, he asked me again, "You sure?"

"Yes," I answered, at the same time I ran my hand over the denim that hid his hard-on.

His eyes fluttered closed, then with a strength that surprised me, he cupped my arse and lifted me onto his waist. My legs instinctively wrapped around him, and I was taller than him like this. I held on around his neck and he knelt on the bed and lowered me onto the mattress, settling himself between my legs.

Oh, fuck.

With both hands on his face, I brought his mouth to mine and kissed him deeply. He bucked his hips into mine, and I needed to get rid of the clothing between us. Not breaking our kiss, I slipped my hands between us and fumbled with his jeans button.

Reed pushed up from me, his kiss-swollen lips smiling, his eyes smouldering desire. He undid his jeans and freed his cock. He was a solid eight inches of uncut glory. I almost came right there.

"Fuck."

"Not today."

My breath hitched, and then he roughly popped the button on my jeans and took out my cock. He hummed appreciatively as he wrapped his hand around me, then leant on his free hand at my shoulder. He aligned our cocks and took them both in his huge hand and never broke eye contact as he pumped us together. His hand, rough and calloused from lifting weights felt divine, his stare was intense and molten blue.

I reached up and cradled his face, delving my tongue into his mouth. He rocked forward with an almighty groan, and I could feel his cock swell and surge against mine as he came. Unable to hold back my orgasm, I quickly followed, coming onto our bellies between us. With the shockwaves still rolling through me, Reed slid his arms underneath me and held me in a perfectly crushing embrace until my orgasm subsided.

He nudged his nose against my jaw and chuckled. "Well, that was over embarrassingly fast."

"That was fucking hot."

He laughed, and his warm breath on my neck sent shivers down my spine. "We should get cleaned up," he murmured. He made no attempt at moving, except to nudge my neck with his nose, then the shell of my ear. It was obvious by my erratic breathing that I liked it, and he chuckled. I ran my hand through his hair and craned my neck to give him more room. He spoke on a sigh, "Or we could stay right here."

I took my time running my hands under his shirt, over his back, tracing lazy circles across his wide shoulders, feeling the strong planes of muscles. It was a new thing for me, and one I found I quite liked. I'd never been with a guy of his stature, but I loved his size, his strength. I loved feeling wrapped up and safe, and that was new for me as well.

Reed pulled back so he could look into my eyes, and he pushed the hair off my forehead. "You okay?"

I couldn't help myself. I had to touch his face. "I'm better than okay."

He gave me his eye-crinkling smile before quickly pressing his lips to mine. "We really are a mess. And I think we're actually physically stuck together."

"If you wanted to shower first...?"

"Is it too soon for you to join me?"

I swallowed hard. "Too soon in the day? Or too soon in whatever this is between us?"

He smirked. "The jizz between us or the relationship between us?"

I burst out laughing. Though I liked the word relationship. Reed's answer was to roll off me, grab my hand, and pull me from the bed. Neither of us stopped to tuck ourselves in; he just led me to the bathroom and turned the shower water on. He turned back to me and, with a grin, reached behind his head and pulled his shirt off.

Jesus. He was shirtless, his cock protruded half-hard, and his jeans were undone but still around his hips, and my come was smeared on his stomach. He couldn't have looked hotter.

"You okay?" he asked.

I was staring, and there was little point to hide it. "You're really fucking beautiful."

He snorted and stepped out of his jeans, revealing his thick, defined thighs. "Okay, so I was wrong. I thought you couldn't get hotter before, but *hello legs*."

Now he laughed. "Your turn."

"I don't have clothes to get changed into."

He looked down. "Your jeans are fine. You can just wear one of my shirts."

And suddenly, I was nervous about being naked with him. Which was ridiculous, considering what we'd just done.

Reed smiled like he knew exactly what I was thinking. He slowly pulled my shirt over my head and turned me around so I faced the bathroom vanity, and of course, the mirror. "Look at yourself, Henry."

I did, though my eyes were drawn straight to his refection behind me. I mean his shoulders were twice as broad as mine. He was a head taller than me. It was hard not to look at him.

"No, look at you," he whispered. I did as he asked, and

Reed studied my chest in the mirror. I wasn't defined like him, or tanned for that matter. I had lost some weight, and I had toned up a little, but it was nothing compared to him. "I like what I see, Henry," he said, planting a kiss on the top of my shoulder. He did seem to like what he saw. He told me he liked me for me, regardless of the body I had. I stared at my reflection, trying to see what he did, and Reed waited until the mirror started to fog up. "Come on, I hate to waste water."

He opened the shower door and stepped under the stream. I shook my head at how fucking absurd this day had been, finished getting undressed, and joined him.

He was already soapy, and if I thought he was hot before, then I would gladly stand corrected. Because him being wet and soapy was a sight that literally took my breath away. I reached up and touched a stream of bubbles that was making its way down between his pecs and onto the defined muscles of his abdominals. Even the bubbles looked happy to be there. Not that I could blame them.

Reed took his shower gel and loofah and scrubbed the mess dried on my belly, then trailed his hands all over me. He wasn't shy about touching me, and I tried not to think about how out of shape I was, especially around my middle. He certainly didn't seem to notice, or care. When I was sufficiently scrubbed, and given there wasn't a great deal of room in his shower, we had to sidestep around each other for me to get under the stream of water. After I was rinsed off, Reed tilted my head back into the spray of water and kissed me.

He pulled away with a devilish smirk and turned off the taps. He stepped out and handed me a towel before quickly drying himself. While he pulled on his jeans, he said, "So, I was thinking..."

I towelled off. "Yeah?"

"Well, I still have all the ingredients for that salad I was going to make you last night. We could do that now, if you like?" He did up his jeans and ran the towel over his hair, making it stick up in all directions. "I'm hungry. But I'm always hungry, so if you'd rather leave it, I can just grab something else."

I pulled on my jeans and did them up, feeling a little less insecure not being completely naked in front of him. "Sure! Sounds great. I'm kinda hungry actually."

He grinned and scooped up our dirty shirts. "Excellent. I'll just go find you a clean one of these."

I hung up both towels, and he appeared a second later with two T-shirts in his hand. They were identical, just like the one he was wearing earlier. A simple cotton shirt with a sports brand across the front, both the same size. Except when he put his on, he filled it like a god, and when I put mine on, it fit me very differently.

Reed just smiled happily, like it made not one lick of difference. "Come on. I need fooooooooood."

He led the way to the kitchen, talking cheerfully as I followed. "The best thing about this recipe is that it takes fifteen minutes." He opened the fridge and rifled through it, handing me ingredients as he found what he needed. "And considering I eat about six times a day, quick meals are a good thing."

"Six times?"

He closed the fridge door with two bottled waters in his hand. "Yep. My metabolism is kinda fast. I burn a lot of calories at work, so I usually just keep fruit and protein bars with me. You'll get used to it." Then he made a face. "If you want to get used to it, that is."

I put the salad stuff on the counter and took one of the bottles of water he was holding. "I would like to get used to it."

He grinned, but he blushed a little as he nodded. "Good. Me too."

And Emily's words came back to me. He might be a big guy, but that doesn't mean he doesn't feel. And while my preconceived stereotyped notion was that all gym junkies were fuck-anything types, he couldn't have been any more opposite. He was just as vulnerable as me.

"I'm glad you like to eat," I said. "Because I like to cook. But just so you know, I have a protein bar you can have any time."

It took him a second, but then he realised what I was talking about. He chuckled. "So you have the sense of humour of a fifteen year old boy."

"Pretty much. You'll get used to it." I took a sip of water. "Oh, and I still have to make you that beetroot thing. It was incredible."

"Okay." He kissed me with smiling lips. "Maybe this afternoon? We could take a walk to Coles later if you want?"

"We could. But I have the ingredients for it at my place."

His gaze met mine, and there was a flicker of heat there. "Sounds good."

It was pretty obvious that my offer for him to have dinner with me was also an invitation for something more physical. I didn't think we were at the having-anal-sex stage yet, but there were about a hundred other things we could do. I realised then that we needed to have the talk.

"So…" I started cautiously. I picked up the sweet potato. "I guess we need to talk about sexual histories and expectations at some point." He looked at the phallic shaped potato in my hand and smirked, and I snorted. "Yes, your apt sized vegetable is apt."

He handed me the peeler, then thought better of it, and took the potato and peeler back. "I might do that part. Can you wash the salad leaves?"

I chuckled but emptied the leaf mix into the salad spinner. "I saw the doctor before I started at the gym, you know, for a health check-up. Everything came back fine. I was with Graham for eight years, and I've only ever practiced safe sex. I can count the guys I've been with on both hands, including you." I let a breath out through puffed out cheeks and tried to not let my embarrassment get the better of me. "I have topped before, but I prefer to bottom. It's just what I like, though I've only ever bottomed for men I've trusted."

Reed stopped peeling the potato and put it on the sink. Without a word, he wiped his hands and stepped over to me, pressing himself right up against me. I had no choice but to look up, and when I did, he kissed me, softly, sweetly. "Thank you for telling me that." He sighed and kissed me chastely again. "I was tested for everything imaginable when I found my ex cheating on me," he said. "I was given the all-clear. I haven't been with anyone since then."

"I'm sorry he did that to you."

"Me too. But I'm glad I found out the truth." He smiled sadly. "Anyway, my history... well, I spent most of my early twenties seeing what my new body could do." He cringed. "Sorry."

I snorted. "Was it like a shiny new toy?"

He nodded quickly. "Uh, yeah. But for about the last six years, I've only ever had sex with guys I've had relationships with. I need that connection." He shrugged now. "Or intimacy just doesn't work for me."

I leaned up on my toes and stretched as tall as I could, and he *still* had to lean down so I could kiss him. It made him smile against my lips, but then his stomach growled.

I pushed him back. "Food. Now."

He chuckled. "I'm trying, but you keep distracting me."

I went back to salad washing and he went back to peeling and slicing the sweet potato. Then he steamed it in the microwave for ten minutes and switched his counter top grill on to heat up. Every now and then he'd stop to touch me or kiss me. He grilled the steamed sweet potato, then the lamb fillets, threw together a salad of mixed leaves and fresh capsicum with a balsamic vinaigrette, served it all up, and we chatted effortlessly about food, music and movies as we ate.

When we moved to the sofa, we sat at opposite ends, and Reed tucked one of his legs up under his arse. He was so relaxed, and he made me feel like I belonged right where I was. He told me some funny stories of his childhood and how wonderful but also embarrassing his family could be. He told me some of the strangest things he'd ever seen in a gym, and I told him of the time Anika had taken me in for a pedicure and we could hear everything that went on in the cubicle next to us. Apparently happy endings were a thing, and Reed laughed, saying sex in the showers in gyms is quite common. "Not at my gym now, but at another one," he clarified. "But just to be sure, I try not to shower at work, and if I have to, I always wear protective footwear."

I hadn't realised that we'd edged closer to each other on the sofa, but we were now sitting side on and facing each other, almost touching. Reed seemed to notice at the same time, and he gently touched my jaw. His gaze went from my jaw to my lips, and when he looked into my eyes, his pupils darkened. He brought our lips together, while his free hand found my hip and he positioned me as he wanted. He pushed me back on the sofa and lay on top of me.

Jesus Christ.

If he kept kissing me like this, I'd be needing a pair of his jeans as well.

He broke the kiss and rested his forehead on my cheek. "I'm sorry. I keep getting carried away," he murmured. "It's been a while for me, and you're so fucking kissable."

I wanted to roll my hips, and I wanted him to take me to bed and bury that huge fucking cock of his inside me. But with the self-control of a monk, I refrained. "Call me Mother Teresa."

He pulled back, startled, like I had some disturbing nun kink. "What?"

I burst out laughing. "No, I just meant I'm trying so hard not to let you fuck me that I'm practically a saint."

"Oh." Then he laughed too, thank God. He climbed off me and scooted to his end of the couch. He let out a steady breath. "I want that too, Henry. But we should wait. We should wait, shouldn't we?"

I sat up and palmed my dick to dampen my arousal. I agreed with a nod. "Yes, that's probably a good idea." And it was. I didn't want to end up in bed only to realise we weren't ready and ruin what could be the beginning of something very amazing. "Physically, I think we're more than ready. Emotionally, I think we could use a few dates, yeah?"

He jumped up to his feet, wearing a smile that could only be described as relieved. He pulled me up so I was standing in front of him. "Thank you for being on the same page." He looked like he might kiss me again but took a step back instead and readjusted the hefty bulge in his jeans. "Jesus. Okay, you can call me Mother Teresa too."

Turning him on was a heady feeling. I swallowed hard. "I think tonight after dinner we can find something else to do," I suggested.

"Such as?"

"Scrabble. Uno. Twister. That kind of thing."

He stared at me.

So I clarified. "And by Scrabble, Uno, and Twister, I really do mean handjobs, blowjobs, and more frottage."

He laughed. "Now those are games I can play."

Then I remembered something. "There's something I need to do first though."

"What's that?"

"I need to drop off some baggage I no longer need."

Reed looked a little confused, but I smiled. And so, with Reed with me, I drove to the nearest charity shop and took the box of Graham's belongings out of the boot. Before I put them in the drop-bin, Reed put his hand on my arm. "Are you sure?"

"I am so sure. I should've done it the day he left."

"But you weren't ready then."

"No. I wasn't. But I am now. To be honest, I should've done it two or three years ago. I guess it needed to run its course for me to get to this point." I shrugged and met his gaze. "I'm happy with where I'm headed. And that's nothing to do with you, Reed. I mean, don't get me wrong, I'm happy with where we're heading too. But I'm happier with who I am and knowing what I want than I have been in years. I want to get fitter and healthier, for me——not for anyone else. I'm not ready to take on the world, but I'm ready to leave this behind." I held up the box.

Reed rewarded me with one of those eye-crinkling smiles and a soft kiss. "Good for you, Henry."

And just like that, I put the box of Graham's things——the things he'd discarded, belongings and memories——into the charity bin, and walked away. I felt lighter, stronger than I ever had.

Reed and I went back to my place, where I made him a late lunch of the beetroot tart, which he devoured, and cooked us a dinner of prawns and linguine. He spent the entire time in the kitchen with me, distracting me with kisses to the back of my neck and breathy sighs in my ear.

And later that night, we played Scrabble, Uno, *and* Twister.

THIRTEEN

I walked into the office on Monday morning with a coffee for me and one for Melinda. I put it on her desk as I breezed in, and she took one look at me, blinked, and stood up. She grabbed her coffee and ushered me into my office, shutting the door behind us. "Oh my God, Henry. Tell me everything." Then she paused and seemed to consider something in mid-air. "Okay, not *every*thing. Spare me the dirty details, but you and Reed. What happened?"

"How do you know something happened?"

She raised one eyebrow at me. "One, you brought me coffee. Two, that ridiculous smile says you got lucky. And three..." She tilted her head. "What are you doing?"

"Trying not to smile."

"Well, stop it. Details, Henry. I want them. Don't make me call Anika."

I laughed and quite possibly did a little dance before taking a self-composing breath. "Yes, Reed and I... cleared the air."

She squealed and jumped, then had to mop spilled coffee off my desk. "Keep talking."

So I told her everything, minus the dirty details.

"So, you're together?"

"Well, yes. I think so."

"As in boyfriends."

"I think so?" I really hadn't asked *that* question. "He didn't stay the whole night, because he has really early starts and all his work stuff was at his place, obviously."

"What do you mean *think so*?"

"Well, we didn't discuss labels. But he is definitely a one-man guy. His ex cheated on him, so he's very pro exclusive. Oh, Melinda, he's just the sweetest guy. And he's gorgeous, and he's utterly perfect."

"No one's perfect," she stated, clearly trying to rain on my parade. "Tell me one of his flaws."

"He has none."

"He has to. Name some."

I tried really hard to think of something I might consider a flaw... "Well, he starts work really early. He's a health-freak, but in a good way. He eats a *lot* of food, but it's like 98 per cent healthy."

"I don't think any of that qualifies as a flaw, Henry."

"He doesn't own any Bee Gee albums."

She gasped and put her hand to her heart. "Do you think that's something you can get past?"

I rolled my eyes. "He just hasn't appreciated the goodness that is Barry Gibb. Yet."

"You will teach him the ways of the falsetto and tight white pants."

"I detect a tone of sarcasm."

"You detect correctly. What else is wrong with him?"

"Who? Reed or Barry Gibb?"

"Reed. I know what's wrong with Barry Gibb."

I sighed, but then I remembered something. "Oh! I know! He's making me do the Bay Run this weekend."

Melinda blinked. "*The* Bay Run."

"Yep. Crazy, huh?"

"A little, yeah."

"I've been practicing, and he says I don't have to jog the whole way. I can run three kilometres without stopping or dying. So I should be okay."

"Three kilometres? Holy shit, Henry. No wonder you're looking so good."

I instinctively went to rebuff her compliment, but after the last weekend of acknowledging my accomplishments with diet and exercise and acknowledging I still had a long way to go, I gave her a smile instead. "Thanks."

Just then my phone rang and Anika's name flashed on the screen. "Oh boy."

"You haven't told her yet?"

"I was kinda busy," I whispered.

Melinda laughed, took her coffee, and went for the door. "I'll hold all calls."

I fell into my chair with a grin and answered my phone. "You want the dirty details? Or the sanitised version I just gave Melinda?"

Anika's response was to squeal and laugh. "Do you even have to ask?"

I WALKED into the gym ten minutes early on Tuesday morning. I never thought I'd ever be excited to exercise, given just five weeks ago I had to drag myself through the doors. Now I walked in with a smile. I couldn't believe how much had changed.

"Hi, Henry," some guy said. I think his name was Dave.

"Good, thanks."

Okay, well, not that much has changed. "I mean, hi. Sorry, not caffeinated yet."

He just laughed and went on his way, and Emily greeted me with a bright and cheery, "Morning." Her smile was a little too knowing.

I tried not to blush. "Morning."

"You're early."

"Yeah, I um, I…"

She nodded. "I know. He won't be long."

I cleared my throat. "Well, yes. Who would've thought I'd be this keen to exercise?"

"Yep. Someone had a little bounce in his step this morning too," she said, looking fondly over at Reed, who was helping a client on the cable and pulley machine. Like he knew we were talking about him, he looked up and smiled when he saw me.

I'm pretty sure I turned a stroke-inducing shade of red. "Oh."

"That's a good thing, Henry," she offered softly. Then, thankfully, she changed subjects. "So, you ready for the Bay Run this weekend?"

"Do you mean, have I prepared my last will and testament?"

Emily laughed at that. "It won't be that bad. And Reed wouldn't have suggested it if he didn't think you could do it."

"We'll see. I should ask though if the ambulance service will drive behind me, you know like they do at the horse races?"

"There's a café about half way."

"Ooh," I brightened. "Coffee. Defibrillation. Same thing really."

"You're not having coffee half way," Reed said, walking over to us. His smile was mesmerising, and I'm pretty sure this was the smile Emily had talked about: the one he saved just for me. It made my heart miss a beat, speaking of defibrillation.

I looked up at him and sighed. "Hey."

He fisted his singlet top at his sides, like it was all he could do not to touch me. "Hey."

"Oh God, you two are just too cute," Emily said. Then she inhaled deeply, like she could smell something bad, and fanned her face. "Oh sweet Jesus, the testosterone. I'm drowning in it. Can you two please resolve the unresolved issue you have going on. You're killing me."

Reed chuckled at her. "You're welcome." Then he nodded pointedly at the treadmills. "You ready to run three Ks?"

"I liked Emily's suggestion better. Just so you know." Unresolved sexual tension was my new favourite thing. Actually, scrap that. Reed's singlet top was my new favourite thing.

Reed pulled on the hem and looked down at it. "You like it?"

"Did I say that out loud?"

"Um, yeah."

"Just the part about the singlet or the part with the sexual tension as well?"

He grinned. "Just the singlet."

"Oh, good. I'd hate for it to be embarrassing or anything."

Reed just grinned, but Emily laughed for a solid five minutes. I think I'd passed the one kilometre mark on the treadmill and she was still chuckling.

Reed stood at my side, looking all relaxed and gorgeous while I puffed and panted and sweated my way through the run. "Looking good, Henry," he said encouragingly. "You're doing it easy."

I waved him off because I couldn't run and talk at the same time. But when the treadmill finally beeped and slowed, I gladly got off and wiped my face down with my towel. My legs were a bit wobbly but nowhere near as bad as they were when I first started this whole exercise fiasco.

"Come sit down," Reed said, leading me toward the weight benches.

"Do I look that bad? Because I know I joke about it, but I don't think I'm actually going to fall over and die."

He smiled and shook his head. "Not at all. I just want you to rest for five minutes before we start with the strength part." He waited for me to sit, then sat beside me. "So, your dinner last night was good?"

We'd texted most of the evening, talking about our day at work. I'd told him of the pumpkin and cranberry bread Dee had brought in for Monday morning tea bring-along and how I'd chatted with her, then Valerie and Fariq, two people at work I'd never spoken to before. I made a stir-fry for dinner and sent him a photo of it. "Yeah it was." His responding picture was of him, legs extended to the coffee table, a bowl of pasta and veggies on his lap. "Though I preferred the look of yours. Your dinner looked good too."

He chuckled, then went quiet for a minute. "Can I ask you something?"

"Of course."

"Are you still happy for me to be your personal trainer?"

I stared at him. "What?"

He looked at his hands in his lap. "I have to ask you, Henry. Now things between us are... personal, if you're comfortable with me still being your trainer?"

Oh. I hadn't thought of how this could complicate his job. "Is it a gym policy that you can't date clients?"

"No, our contract says we should be professional with members at all times."

"You've been very professional with me."

He gave me a kind smile and whispered, "I've also been very personal."

"Does it bother you?"

"Not at all. But if you'd prefer, I can find someone else to be your trainer."

I shook my head. "I don't prefer."

"Because I want to keep seeing you outside of work, Henry, if you know what I mean. But you already missed your session on Sunday because of me. So if you'd prefer——"

"I prefer you. As my trainer and as my... whatever you are. I don't know what we are, technically. But I like it. I like you as both, and I don't want to choose. I didn't miss out on anything on Sunday. Actually, Sunday was kinda great, if I recall. And anyway, I wouldn't have made it this far with this whole fitness debacle if it weren't for you, and I wouldn't have realised that it's okay to be me, just the way I am, if you weren't my... whatever you are. I'm not good with labels. But I want you for both."

He looked right at me, his gaze melting into me. "I want you for both too." He studied his hands again, though this time a smile formed at the corners of his lips. "And just so you know, Sunday was great for me too. And if it's alright with you, I could come around to your place for dinner tonight? I don't have to work tomorrow, and we could work on what label to give whatever this is."

I grinned at him. "I'd like that."

He took a deep breath, like a weight had been lifted from his shoulders. "Excellent. Now, let's get started with some lateral holds, tricep curls, and shoulder presses."

"Ugh. Can I renege on my invitation for dinner?"

He chuckled. "Nope. Because I invited myself."

"That's just a technicality."

"Maybe. But it works."

"And just so I'm clear, when you say you don't have to work tomorrow, were you implying you don't have to be up early?"

He glanced around quickly, and when he was sure no one could hear him, he said, "That, or that I don't have to leave tonight."

I swallowed hard at the thought of him sleeping in my bed, and a warm rush of blood surged to my groin. It made me squirm. "Is that another technicality?"

He smirked like he knew the answer already. "Does it work?"

"Yes," I answered way too quickly. I wouldn't apologise for my excitement. He should just be grateful I didn't answer with interpretive dance. "Yes it does."

Reed set the weights on the machine for me. "Good. Now get these done. You've got fifteen minutes left. If we keep cutting into your training time, you won't be ready for this weekend."

I stood at the machine, feet apart, and pulled the weights in a lateral hold. "I'm pretty sure we can add cardio of some description to our plans tonight."

He smiled mischievously. "I'm sure we can."

Someone came over and asked him something about the rowing machine, and we never got another chance to talk alone. Not that I minded. It was his place of employment, after all, and I respected his job. I finished the reps he told me to do and waved goodbye as I left.

I got to work feeling energised. I had heard people talk about having more energy when they'd exercised, and if I was truthful, I'd always rolled my eyes while thinking it would be impossible to have *more* energy when it was obvious exercise, like walking up a flight of steps, would try to kill me.

But it was true. I did have more energy. I was sleeping better, I was drinking more water than ever, and I was generally feeling a hundred per cent better than I did two months ago.

At lunchtime, I made Melinda come with me to buy new work clothes. I just couldn't get away with cinching in my work pants anymore. They were starting to look like pantaloons. I had to bribe her with sushi, but it was totally worth it. I needed an honest opinion, and if anyone wore honesty like a well-fitted suit, it was Melinda.

The pretty suit-tailor guy looked me up and down with his Judgy MacJudgerson eyes, and before I could tell him I was a better bottom than he could ever be, he clicked his fingers. "Thirty-eight."

"I'm thirty five, fuck you very much."

He blinked, and Melinda put her hand on my arm. "Size thirty eight, Henry."

"Oh." I lifted my chin. "Sorry." Then it sunk in what he said. Size thirty-eight? No freakin' way. I hadn't been a size thirty-eight in years. I turned to Melinda and tried not to butt-wiggle. I might have squealed. "Thirty-eight!"

I had only intended to buy one suit, but one blue suit, one grey, and one charcoal suit later, we walked back to the office. Despite the damage to my bank account, I was still buzzing. In fact, I was too excited to wait for the elevators, so I made Melinda take the stairs with me.

She collapsed in her chair, and I held up my shopping bags and twirled. "Size thirty-eight!"

"Dying."

"It was only four flights."

"I hate you."

"But size thirty-eight!"

She waved me off, mumbling under her breath something that I'm pretty sure ended with "... before I kill you."

I pointed to my office door. "I have work to do." She replied with a glare that could scare a cat, and I walked into my office, not scared of her at all. Much.

I sent a spray of size thirty-eight texts to Anika. I sent a selfie of me, holding the size thirty-eight suit tag smiling like an idiot to Reed, then I even sent a quick text to my mum asking how her day was going.

Anika's response was all in shouty caps. *YOU SKINNY BASTARD. I WANNA BE SKINNY TOO BUT I LOVE FRAPPES. DID I MENTION SKINNY BASTARD? AND NOW I WANT A FRAPPE.*

Reed's response was much more subdued. *So proud of you. I'll be at yours at seven. That okay?*

I quickly typed out a reply. *I'll be home by five thirty...*

See you at six.

I might have hugged my phone.

Then my mother replied with a voice message. "Henry, dear, you know I don't know how these phones work. Is this being made into a text? How does it know what I'm saying? Anyway, how's your new beau doing? He was very hand-some. And tall. When will you be coming over for dinner? You will bring him, yes? Oh, and you know Marilyn from bingo? Well, her daughter said that George Clooney——" The phone beeped in my ear, cutting off her message, and I could imagine my mother sitting there still talking, telling me all about her friends until she realised the voice mail had ended God knows how long ago. I made a mental note to write down, in point form this time, how to reply to a text. And it might be time to recap on the whole "Mum, George Clooney is married now" conversation we had just six months ago.

I spent my afternoon buried in financial statistics, and even that couldn't dampen my mood. And I spent the car trip home wondering what on earth I should cook for dinner tonight. When I got home and changed my clothes, I rifled through my fridge and pantry for ideas on what to cook, but came up uninspired.

There was a knock on the door, right on six o'clock. I opened the door to find Reed smiling at me, and I had to wonder if this day could possibly get any better. "Why yes, I do believe I'll have whatever it is you're selling," I joked.

I didn't even realise he had one hand behind his back, but with a grin, he revealed a single rose. "I'm not selling it. It's a gift. From me to you."

"Oh." I think my heart melted into a bubble of useless goo. "Thank you. No one has ever given me a flower before."

I took the rose and he stepped inside, giving me a kiss on the lips. "You're welcome. I figured if I invited myself for dinner, it was the least I could do."

"I'm glad you invited yourself for dinner, but I have a confession."

"What's that?"

"I have no idea what to cook."

"We can just order in if you want?"

I shook my head. "Nope. You know what I feel like?" I didn't give him time to answer. "Poached fish with lemongrass and ginger."

"Okay then."

"Fancy a trip to the supermarket with me?"

He chuckled. "I bring you a rose and you take me to Coles?"

"Romantic, huh?" I grinned at him. I held up the single most perfect rose in the world and inhaled the scent of it. "Let me just put this in some water, and I'll grab my keys."

Five minutes later, we walked into the supermarket. Reed grabbed a basket and we headed for the seafood section. Normally I'd go to the fish markets, but this would have to do. I selected the best red snapper fillets they had on offer, then we grabbed some fresh ginger, chilli, and limes.

"Come this way," Reed said, nodding toward the freezer section.

By his smirk, I knew he was up to no good, and when he stopped at the ice-cream selections, I gawped at him. "Do you know how good I've been? I've been having my weekly treat on Mondays at work, and yesterday's morning tea was pure carbs and fat, and delicious by the way, and you want to kill me with ice cream?"

Reed opened the freezer door and picked out a pack of two little individual tubs. "These are gelato, and they're tiny. It's like two mouthfuls, and they'll be perfect after dinner."

I raised an eyebrow at him. "You don't have some weird kink where you get off by feeding fat people, do you?"

Reed burst out laughing. "No! I swear. You don't have to get them. I just thought it'd be nice to cleanse the palate after ginger and chilli, that's all."

I sighed dramatically. "Alright then. If you insist. But if my new size thirty-eight suits don't fit me in the morning, I'll blame you."

He threw the gelatos into the basket. "That's fine. I'll just make you do a 5K run on Thursday."

I pushed his shoulder. "Fuck you."

He laughed some more when someone behind us spoke. "Henry?"

I turned around and stopped cold. Graham stood there, looking at me like he couldn't believe his eyes. "Graham," I replied, more for Reed's benefit than his.

Reed edged a little closer to me, which I had to admit, I really fucking liked. I watched as Graham looked up Reed's chest to his face then jolted his head, like he had to physically make himself look at me. I was only wearing jeans and a sweater, but Graham would have undoubtedly recognised the jeans that hadn't fit me in years. "You look good, Henry."

"Thanks," I said, disregarding the compliment because coming from him, I had to wonder about the sincerity. "You look..." exactly the same, except for the excess hair product, and wait, is that hair dye? I cleared my throat. "So do you." I couldn't lie for shit, and we both knew it.

Graham looked up at Reed again and gave him a sleazy smile. "The name's Graham Martin," he said, holding his hand out. *Dear God, was he trying to come onto him? In front of me?*

Reed shook Graham's hand, and I had to wonder what it took for Graham not to flinch with how strong Reed gripped his palm. "Reed Henske," he said flatly. It was pretty clear Reed didn't like him. It made me smile.

"So...?" Graham hedged, looking between Reed and me. "You two are...?"

"Boyfriends," Reed answered. "Well, we're working on it."

Well, I guess that took care of the label dilemma I had earlier. I had wondered what to call him or to call whatever our relationship was. Reed just answered that question, leaving no room for doubt. I had to bite the inside of my lip so I didn't smile too much. *Boyfriends. Holy shit.*

Graham's gaze shot to mine. "Right. Well, I guess that's... Good for you, Henry."

And it struck me, right in the middle of aisle two of Coles that I didn't want to be a bitch about this. I spent eight years of my life with him, and we were adults. "I should thank you, Graham. I mean, I didn't realise it at the time, but you leaving was the wake-up call I needed. Neither of us were happy and weren't for a long time. I can see that now."

He seemed a little surprised by my honesty, but his eyes softened. "I'm glad it's working out for you."

"Are you happy?"

He gave a bit of a nod. "Yeah." I didn't know whether to believe him or not, but it was no longer my place to say. "And I'm sorry I never replied to your text."

"I gave your stuff to charity," I said. "Anika wanted to set fire to it, but I wouldn't let her. I was tempted, though."

Graham almost smiled. "Yeah, I guess I deserved that."

My "hell yes you did" went unsaid. I turned to Reed and put my hand on his side. "We should get going, yeah?" He gave a nod, so I looked at Graham. "It was good to see you."

"Same," he replied. "And you really do look good, Henry."

We left him there in the middle of the cold aisle——the irony of that was not lost on me——and Reed put his arm around my shoulders. I had no doubt Graham was still watching us, so I put my arm around Reed's waist as we headed for the checkouts. "You okay?" Reed asked.

I gave him a bit of a squeeze. "Never better."

We loaded the few groceries into my car and went back to my place. Reed was a little quiet, and I knew there was something we needed to address. I put the grocery bags on the counter and wasted no time. "I'm sorry you met him," I said. "And I'm sorry if it made you feel uncomfortable."

"No, it's not that," he said. "I kinda behaved like a jerk. Sorry."

"No you didn't."

"Well yeah, I did. You were mature about it, and all I could think was that he's been with you, and he knows things about you that I don't." He frowned. "That sounds really bad, doesn't it?"

I closed the distance between us and leaned up on my toes in an attempt to kiss him. I still couldn't reach, so I slid my hand around his neck and pulled him down to meet me. It made him smile. "It doesn't sound bad. It sounds honest. And yes, I have a history with him. I can't change that. But seeing him tonight made me realise he's the last person on the planet that I want to be with. What I had with him is well and truly over."

He finally smiled. "He's not what I pictured him to be like," Reed mused. "I wasn't expecting black hair."

"Did you see the hair dye? I can assure you, he didn't have

that when we were together. Dark hair, yes. A little grey even, but that dye job was bad." I put my hand to Reed's chest. "Jokes aside, I want him to be happy. I don't want anyone to be *un*happy. But my happiness isn't with him, it's with you."

He put his hand under my chin and lifted my face so he could softly press his lips to mine. "I wasn't kidding when I said we were working on the boyfriend thing. Was that okay? Or too much?"

I laughed and put his hand to my chest. "Definitely not too much."

His eye-crinkling smile made my stomach somersault. "Good."

"And just so you know, if we happen to run into your cheating ex-bastard, I won't be as civil as you were with Graham." Reed laughed, but then his stomach growled. "Okay, okay, I'll start cooking."

I filled a pot with water and set it to boil, then added baking paper to my bamboo steamer. I placed the fish inside, and as I chopped the chilli and ginger and got the sauce cooking, Reed sorted out the rice in the microwave cooker and steamed some bok choy and button squash. We worked well as a team in the kitchen, and while I made sure everything was cooking to perfection, Reed stood behind me and pressed his lips to the back of my neck.

"We won't be eating tonight if you keep doing that," I warned, though I'm sure the tone of my voice spurred him on to keep doing it. "Well, there might be shots of protein..."

He chuckled against my neck and pressed himself against my back, his hands on my hips, and his groin firm against my arse. I'm not sure which of us groaned the loudest, and I contemplated leaving all the food to burn while I took him into my bedroom. The microwaved beeped, and he growled in frustration and shivered with disappointment.

"Rice is done," he said. When I glanced over at him, he

was standing at the far end of the kitchen, leaning against the counter, his eyes were a little dark and there was a bulge in his jeans. "I'm staying over here or dinner will be ruined."

I chuckled, but the static in the kitchen bloomed to almost-suffocating levels. I adjusted my cock, which made his nostrils flare. I had to swallow my desire so I could speak. "Plates are just to your left."

I served up two plates of fish, rice, and steamed veggies, while Reed found the cutlery and two bottles of water. Sitting at the table opposite him seemed to quell the sexual tension a little, until he took a bite and made a noise that went straight to my cock.

"Oh my God, Henry. This is so good."

And it was. With each bite, a burst of flavour hit my tongue. "I didn't know healthy could taste so good."

He chuckled and savoured his mouthful. And just like that, the tension between us simmered a little. Enough for us to eat, anyway. When he pushed his plate away, he patted his belly and sighed contentedly. "Absolute perfection. Though my lips are tingling from the chilli."

They did look a little pinker than normal, and my mind fell to the gutter when his tongue peeked out and ran across his top lip. By the look in his eye, he did it deliberately. "Here, let me take these," he said with a smirk, collecting the empty plates. He just happened to stand really close to me, so the fly of his jeans was level with my face.

Bastard.

He laughed as he walked into the kitchen, which made me believe I might have said that out loud.

When he didn't return straight away, I followed him in to find him stacking things into the dishwasher. "You didn't have to do that."

"It's done now." He closed the dishwasher door and stood up straight. "Gelato in front of the TV?"

"Perfect."

He collected the little tubs from the freezer, I grabbed the spoons, and we both fell onto the sofa. He sat at one end, me at the other. At first I was a little disappointed at the distance between us. I didn't know why he sat a full metre away from me, but the way he eye fucked me made me very glad he did.

When I put the spoon in my mouth and tasted the passionfruit gelato, I moaned like a two-dollar whore. I couldn't even be embarrassed because Reed let out a low breath. "Jesus, Henry. I'm trying to be a gentleman here."

I laughed. "Sorry. But this is really good." I was already at the bottom of mine. "You weren't kidding when you said they were two mouthfuls. I'm now regretting not getting a bigger tub."

Reed slid over and took my empty gelato cup. He was so much closer now, his body heat was heady, and he leaned in and ran his nose along my jaw. "If you want something more..."

I shot off the lounge, grabbed his hand, and dragged him to my room. He started to laugh until I pushed him onto the bed and straddled him. "Oh Henry," he murmured, pulling my hips onto his. The denim between us did little to hide his erection, and I loved that I turned him on.

I kissed him, hard, until he was bucking his hips, searching for more friction. Only when he was impatient and breathless, did I kiss down his neck and shuffle down his body. I lifted his shirt up, revealing his perfectly sculptured abs and the wide planes of his chest. I flicked his nipple with my tongue and he hissed, and he gently pulled my hair.

"Oh, fuck."

I kissed down the centre of his six-pack to his navel and sat back to undo his jeans. I popped the button, undid the fly, and gently released his cock. God, it made my mouth water.

"Henry, please."

So I licked him, his length, the head, the slit. His scent was pure musk and man, and it kicked my desire up a notch. I wrapped my fingers around his base and slipped my lips around him, moaning as I took him in.

He carded his fingers through my hair and rolled his hips. "God, your mouth." A groan rumbled in his chest. "Feels so good."

His cock was long and thick, veined with a bulbous head, and as I slid it into my throat, I could almost imagine what it would be like sliding into my arse. God, I ached for it.

I wanted to feel him stretch me, fill me, own me. I wanted to be his, in every sense of the word. God, I needed him inside me. I swallowed around him and swirled my tongue up his shaft as I pulled off. "I can't wait to feel you inside me."

And that was all it took. "I'm gonna come."

I took him in deep once again, just in time to feel him swell and surge in my mouth. He arched his back off the bed and gave a strangled cry as he filled my mouth. I drank everything he gave me, making him moan and writhe. Eventually he let out a low, breathy chuckle. "Jesus, Henry."

I kissed the soft skin above his pubic hair, then gently nipped at those epic muscles at his sides above his hips. He squirmed and laughed. "What are these called?" I asked, kissing the exact spot on both sides.

Reed leaned up to look down at himself, his six-pack flexed under his skin as he did. "Those are a result of working the transverse abdominals, internal and external obliques. They don't really have a name."

"Yes they do. They're called the V muscles, and I'm pretty sure it's what put the V in heaven. Anyway, they're my new favourite thing." Then I kissed up his muscled ribs and licked his nipples, making the dark flesh pebble at the touch. "No, wait. These are my new favourite thing."

He barked out a laugh, then before I knew which way was

up, he flipped me over, pressed himself between my thighs and pinned my hands above my head. "Your turn," he whispered against my lips. "Now let me show you my new favourite thing." He smirked and kissed me softly. "Here." Then my jaw. "Here." My throat. "Here." He pulled my shirt up and kissed my chest, my stomach, my navel. "Here. Here. Here."

I couldn't even be self-conscious. True, I didn't like anyone seeing my naked belly, let alone touching it and even worse, kissing it. But he was so reverent, so honest, that I trusted him impeccably.

He undid my jeans and pulled them off my legs without any effort at all. And when he took my erection from my briefs, I was so turned on, I didn't care about the insecure parts of me. "And here," he murmured. When he took my cock into his warm, wet mouth, I lost all inhibitions, all coherent thought.

He slid his hand inside my briefs, rolling my balls with deft fingers before sliding them as far in as the fabric would allow. His blunt finger traced my perineum, he sucked me harder, and I couldn't hold back any longer.

I came hard enough that my head spun, my body shook, and my hands trembled. Reed was soon lying beside me, and he pulled me into his arms while my orgasm subsided. He kissed the side of my head and nuzzled his nose into my hair. I couldn't keep my eyes open for a second longer.

I woke up at about three o'clock in the morning with a start, until I remembered the huge warm body in my bed was Reed. He was sleeping soundly with his back to me, and I couldn't help but marvel at the sight of him in my bed. Motionless, the moonlight made his back and shoulders look as if they were carved of marble. A sculptor's masterpiece on the perfection of the human body. I gently ran my hand over his muscled frame, feeling the strength and purpose there, even in sleep.

He stirred and rolled over to face me, mumbling something and lifting his arm in invitation. So I snuggled into him, and he wrapped his arm around me, settling straight back into sleep. I kissed his chest with smiling lips and fell into a dream of safety and strength, warmth and wonder.

Fourteen

I woke up before Reed and slipped out of bed to shower. It was his day off, and given the physical nature of his job, I wanted him to enjoy a sleep in. I should've known his stomach would wake him, because as I was making his breakfast, he surprised me in the kitchen.

And by surprised, I mean made my jaw hit the floor. Wearing only his jeans slung low on his hips, he was shirtless and sleep rumpled with stubble and mussed hair. It was the stuff of dreams. And porn.

I stood there with a slice of toast halfway to my hanging-open mouth. He smirked and swiped my toast, biting into it. "Good morning."

"Yes it is." I mean, there was no point in lying about it. It was a fucking great morning. "I was making you breakfast," I added, nodding to the tray on the counter with a coffee and juice and an empty plate. "Just waiting on your toast."

He held up the piece he took from me. "Have some, thanks."

I snorted. "You're welcome."

He chuckled then sighed happily. "Thank you. It was very thoughtful."

"You know, you dressed like that is a good enough reason for me to call in sick."

"Tempted, huh?"

Just then the toast popped up. I grabbed it and buttered it for him. "I would, but I have a video conference meeting today that I probably shouldn't miss. Vegemite okay?"

He sipped his juice and nodded. "Perfect, thanks." When I handed it to him, he looked me up and down. "The suit looks good."

It was hard not to believe him with the heat in his eyes and the gruff tone of his voice. "Oh." I'm pretty sure I blushed. "Thanks."

"I didn't think I'd ever be into the corporate actuary look, but you do it so well."

I had to put my coffee on the counter before I spilled it down the front of me. "There's a corporate actuary look?"

Reed grinned as he chewed his toast. "Yep."

"Is that a nice way to say I'm a boring suit?"

He chuckled. "You're far from boring, Henry. And I like you in your suit. It fits you well."

"I could probably miss that conference call," I mused. "It's just a national one, oh and a few offices throughout Asia. I'm sure it won't be too important."

Reed laughed. "You're not missing work on my account."

"But technically, I wouldn't *miss* it, at all, because what we'd be doing instead would be so much more fun."

"Nice try."

"Are you making me go to work?"

He finished his juice and leaned his entire front against me so he could put his empty glass in the sink. "Yep."

I mumbled into his chest, "You don't play fair."

He laughed and stood back, only to fix my necktie. "You better go if you don't want to be late."

I had to adjust my now-aching dick. "Thanks for giving me something to think about all day."

He grinned proudly. "You're welcome."

I rolled my eyes, though I couldn't help but smile. "I'll drop you home on my way, if you want?"

"Okay. Just let me get dressed."

Ten minutes later, I pulled up at his apartment complex. "I'll call you. And probably text you as well," he said. He opened his door but didn't move to get out. "Thank you. For dinner last night and for breakfast this morning."

"Anytime."

"So, I was thinking maybe we could do it again on Friday night?"

"Sounds good."

"But I'll see you Friday morning for your usual gym session."

"Yes you will."

He leaned across the console and licked his lips before kissing me sweetly. "You smell really good," he murmured. "Just how important is that conference call?"

I laughed. "Get out of my car."

I left him on the footpath with a smile and a promise to talk later, and before I turned onto Darling Street, I called Anika. I told her all about my night, including running into Graham in Coles. "Reed said we were boyfriends and that I smell really good, and he really likes my suit, and I'm pretty sure he wanted me to spend the day with him."

"He told Graham all of that?"

"No, just the boyfriend part. All the rest was later."

"Henry, you know what this means?"

"What?"

"I need to meet him."

"Oh."

"It's my obligatory right as your best friend."

I drove a block in silence.

"Henry? You still there?"

"Yes. Just doing a mental step-by-step of worst case scenarios."

Anika laughed. "It won't be that bad."

"I really like him, Neeky," I whispered.

Her reply was just as soft. "I know you do."

"This Sunday," I suggested, "at the Bay Run. You can be there as they carry me across the finish line on an ambulance stretcher. You can meet him then."

"Deal. Text me the details."

"Of what? My private health cover details? The ambulance fees are included."

She snorted. "No, the details of the run."

"Oh. Okay."

"Love you, Henry."

"Love you, too."

I WAS GOING to tell Reed that Anika wanted to meet him in one of our many texts or phone calls but figured it would be best done face to face. He'd been sequestered to have dinner with his parents on Thursday, so I didn't get to see him until Friday morning when I arrived at the gym.

"Last training session before the big Bay Run this weekend," Emily said as I walked in.

Ugh. "There was no newfound Mayan calendar that predicted the end of the world on Sunday morning by any chance?"

"Nope. Not that I've seen."

"That's a shame."

She chuckled. "It won't be that bad."

"Oh well, it's not the actual run that scares me now. My best friend wants to meet Reed on Sunday."

"Oh."

"Yeah. I should ask him if he has a mouthguard and shin pads. I don't think he'll need them, and truthfully Anika's not a violent person. I'm sure she'll love him. She's just protective of me, that's all."

Emily nodded slowly, while trying not to smile. "I'm pretty sure Reed can hold his own."

"Reed can hold his what?" Reed asked from beside us. His smile was as much curious as it was cautious. "Do I even want to know what you're talking about?"

I tried to reassure him. "Oh, it's not that bad. Do you have life insurance?"

He blanched. "Uh..."

Emily laughed. "Maybe I should go for backup."

By now Reed was looking a little lost and a bit scared, so I explained, "Anika wants to meet you, that's all."

"Oh," he said with a relieved exhale. "Yeah of course. That's fine. When?"

"Sunday, after the Bay Run of death. Look at it this way," I added, "if I do happen to die before I finish, you'll be off the hook."

Reed laughed and led me toward the treadmills. "You're not going to die. And if it makes you feel any better, I had to answer a hundred questions about you to my folks. I'm not saying you'll need a mouthguard when you meet my mum, just that she can make the Spanish Inquisition look like amateurs day."

Before I could really process that he was talking about me

meeting his parents, he hit the Start button on the treadmill and made me run three kilometres. Then I had to do a fifty-calorie climb on the elliptical, and then he made me drag my sweaty, lifeless body over to the free weights for a cool-down.

"You're really focused today," he said. He was looking at me weirdly. "You okay?"

I puffed, still trying to catch my breath. "Focused? Um, no, just trying not to die."

He smiled, apparently able to read me better than I thought. "I told my mum we weren't ready for that just yet. I told her if she absolutely had to meet you today, I would have no problem with that, but maybe we could just go at our own pace. She was happy then."

"Oh."

"That okay?"

I nodded. My breathing had steadied somewhat. "Yeah. Perfect. Actually, my mum might have said something similar, but I just didn't go there. I mean, you have technically met her, but not in a boyfriend capacity. That still sounds kinda weird to say out loud, just so you know. But if you really want me to introduce you to her, she waits at the Nespresso café in the city for George Clooney every Sunday."

He burst out laughing. "I'll keep that in mind."

"So you're really okay with meeting Anika? I promise she'll be on her best behaviour."

"Henry, it's fine." He checked his watch. "But you better get to work."

"We still on for dinner tonight?"

"Hell yes. Pasta and a movie with you. Sounds perfect. Though I do have to be at work by six tomorrow morning, so I'll need to be in bed pretty early."

I cleared my throat. "I have no problem with that."

He was still smiling when I left.

SUNDAY MORNING CAME AROUND TOO FAST. I woke up part excited, part dreading what I was about to do. I'd never imagined I would attempt a seven kilometre anything, but there I was doing ridiculous things like eating a sensible breakfast and pulling on my running shoes. I had trust in Reed's expertise and his faith in me to be able to do this. But just to be on the safe side, I took a final look around my house and watered the plants in case I was hospitalised for any length of time.

I called into the gym to pick Reed up. He was just finishing up his session with Nadia, who had graciously swapped with me so Reed would be free to do the Bay Run.

"Good luck, Henry," Nadia said as she was leaving.

"You got this, Henry," Dave chimed in.

Emily clapped me on the back. "See you on the other side."

I wasn't sure if she meant the other side of mortality. "I'll be the one walking into the light."

She burst out laughing. "Not that other side."

"Shame. I was looking forward to seeing my two childhood pet cats again. Andy and Robin really understood me."

"Andy and Robin?" Emily asked, amused. "From Winnie the Pooh?"

"No. The Bee Gees." *God, didn't these people know anything?*

Everyone within hearing distance laughed just as Reed came over with a bottle of water in his hand. He seemed to pick up on my discomfort and quickly came to stand by my side. "You ready for this?"

"Not at all. And just so you know, I want "Staying Alive" played at my funeral. You know, for irony and laughs."

Reed chuckled and took my hand, pulling me out the door, and when we were outside, he put his arm around my shoulders. If anyone in the gym had wondered about him being a little chummier with me than his other clients, they wouldn't be wondering now. It gave me a thrill that he was open to public displays of affection. Not that I expected him to snog me in the car park, but it also told me he wasn't embarrassed to be seen with me.

And for a guy like me, that meant a lot.

"You're not going to die, Henry. I promise. I'll be running with you, and I know CPR."

I unlocked my car and was just about to speak when he cut me off. "And no, you can't fake unconsciousness so I'll give you mouth-to-mouth."

My shoulders sagged. I had no clue how he knew what I was about to ask. "Oh."

He laughed as he got into my car, and when I pulled the car into the easy Sunday traffic, he held my hand all the way to Drummoyne. It was a shame it was only a five-minute drive, because I really liked the feeling.

I found a parking spot near the rowing club and was met by a crazy woman madly waving from the park. "Oh, there's Anika," I said. I shot Reed a nervous look. "You ready for this?"

He snorted. "I am."

With my heart in my mouth, we crossed the street and headed toward where it appeared that Anika had set up a picnic setting worthy of a photo shoot. She had blankets spread out, several picnic baskets, cushions, and a soft-looking throw rug. And as always, she looked gorgeous. "Jeez, did you spare anything?"

Anika kissed my cheek. "There are benefits to working for Myer, dear."

Sean appeared, carrying more things from the car. "Tell me about it. Do you know how many trips to the car I've had to do?" He put down what looked a small, portable fridge. He straightened up and took a better look at me. "Shit, Henry. You look good."

"Oh, thanks," I said. I swear, taking compliments would never get easier. "Um, guys, this is Reed. Reed, this is Anika and Sean."

Anika's face was priceless. She looked at his chest then up to his face, and there might have been eyelash fluttering. "Hello," she said meekly, holding out her hand. Dear God, what was wrong with her?

Sean looked at Anika like he was thinking the same thing I was thinking, then he shook Reed's hand. "G'day. How's it going?"

"Good, thanks," Reed answered with a smile.

"Sorry about Anika. It's not often she's rendered speechless."

Anika seemed to snap out of whatever daze she was in and lightly whacked Sean's arm. "Shut up."

He just laughed. "No wait, there she is."

She sighed indignantly and seemed to gather her composure. She looked up at Reed. "So, you're the one who has Henry looking like a million dollars?"

"Oh God," I mumbled.

Reed chuckled. "Not sure I can take all the credit."

She held his gaze. "But you're making him run this... marathon?"

"It's not a marathon," I interjected.

"Yes, I am," Reed stated proudly. "Because he doubts himself at every turn, and I want to prove to him that he can do it."

This seemed to please Anika. "Well, good." Then, not taking her eyes off Reed, she directed her question to Sean. "Did you get everything out of the car, dear?"

Sean rolled his eyes behind her back. "Yes, dear."

Reed coughed to hide his laugh, and Anika turned to face Sean, but he was saved by someone walking over to us.

"Melinda?" I asked. I couldn't believe she was here.

She was wearing a knee-length navy plaid skirt, white shirt, and a navy vest, with her usual John Lennon glasses on the end of her nose.

"You don't think I would let you do this without me being here to watch?" she asked.

"Aw, thank you," I said. It meant a lot that she was here to support me.

She gave me a small, pleased smile, then looked up at Reed. She was possibly half his size. "And you must be Reed. Just so you know, Henry made me climb four flights of stairs the other day. I almost died, and I blame you for this. It's nice to meet you, by the way."

She held out her hand, which Reed looked a bit scared to shake. He did it anyway. "Sorry about the exercise."

I made a late introduction. "Yes, sorry. Reed, this is my personal assistant, Melinda. She is a godsend. I'd be lost without her."

Melinda smiled cheerfully, and Anika kissed her cheek. "Hi, darling. Glad you made it."

"Oh," Melinda said, reaching into her satchel. She pulled out some kind of Japanese graphic novel and handed it to Sean. "For you."

Sean's eyes lit up. "Thank you!" He soon made himself comfortable lying down on cushions, already turning to page one. "I'll just stay here until you boys get back."

Oh right. The whole run thing. I almost forgot.

Reed chuckled beside me. "You ready?"

"Not at all."

Reed took my hand. "You're not going to die, Henry."

"I might, then all these outdoor-type people innocently

enjoying the park would be scarred for life. I mean, really, we should think of the children." Melinda snorted and Anika laughed. I tried to glare at them, but then I remembered something. "Oh, and in the case of my untimely and horribly tragic death, you know what song to play at my funeral, right, girls?"

Anika and Melinda answered in unison. "'Staying Alive.'"

Sean laughed, and Reed chuckled as he put his arm around my shoulders and led me back to the path that wrapped around the bay.

Reed made me stretch for a few minutes before we started.

"Your friends are great," he said. "Very funny. I can see why you all get along."

"Anika is like my twin. We think the same. And Melinda... well, don't let the innocent schoolgirl look fool you. She's secretly a mathematical genius ninja and can kill four different ways with chopsticks."

Reed burst out laughing. "Must make your job interesting."

"Never a dull moment," I answered. "With any of them."

"And Anika seems to like me?" He seemed unsure. "It didn't go too bad, did it?"

"It went well. Though you can probably expect the 'hurt him and I'll kill you' speech when she gets you alone."

"Fair enough," he said with a smile. "Emily read you the riot act, didn't she?"

"Yes, though I was very brave."

Reed smiled and looked down the path we would soon be taking. "Okay, so we're going to jog, slow and steady, for three kilometres."

I whined.

"You do it three times a week, Henry. And we're gonna do it at your pace."

"My pace is about fifty kilometres an hour, in my car."

Reed chuckled, and with a nod over his shoulder, he said,

"Come on. Let's do this."

And so I did. I started off on the seven kilometre Bay Run, with the only person on the planet who could have ever made me think it was possible.

FIFTEEN

REED KNEW I COULDN'T JOG AND TALK AT THE SAME time, so he stayed alongside me, the support in his silence loud and clear.

The path that traced the bay was for joggers and cyclists, dog-walkers and pram pushers. It was very scenic and a popular place to be. But in the past, I'd simply driven on the road next to them, never given any of them a single thought.

Now under a perfect Sydney sky, they smiled at us or gave a nod or a "hi" as we went past each other. I had to admit, it was nice and reaffirming that society, and people in general, didn't all suck like I'd presumed for years.

I wasn't miraculously cured of my cynicism, but the change of outlook, no matter how brief, was refreshing.

Don't get me wrong, I was still dying. And I'd never been more relieved when Reed's phone beeped. He pressed a button and said, "That's three Ks. Wanna keep going?"

I stopped and waved my hand dramatically before putting my hands on my knees and gulping in air. "No. Dying. Fuck. Legs. Lungs. On. Fire."

Reed was barely sweating. "You're doing great. And you're almost halfway. Come on, keep walking."

We'd probably walked a hundred metres before I could talk properly. "It's different than running on a treadmill."

"It is."

"It's harder."

"Treadmills are a controlled environment. This isn't." He looked at his watch again, and pressed some more buttons. "Come on. This time we'll go for one K."

And so we jogged again. I was nearly taken out by a guy on a bike, and Reed had to pull on my elbow to avoid me being mowed down by a lady pushing a stroller, who I was certain was being remote-controlled by the evil toddler in the stroller. The little kid laughed when I almost tripped over but miraculously managed not to face plant. I considered giving the kid the bird, but thought it might be frowned upon.

Somehow, I made that one kilometre, then we walked for a bit while I caught my breath. Before I knew it, we were around the other side of the bay, and I could see the Haberfield Rowing Club up ahead. "Jesus."

Reed smiled effortlessly and showed me his watch. "Less than two kilometres to go."

I had a sip of water. "And I'm not even dead yet."

"Not even close," he replied. And so we started to run again. Well, maybe the word run was a little ambitious. At the rate we were being overtaken by people with prams and dogs, it was safe to assume the term *slow jog* was probably more apt.

But I didn't stop for another kilometre.

This time I needed to not walk. I needed to stop completely and take some deep breaths. With my hands on my hips, I had to work to get air into my already struggling lungs.

Reed gave my shoulder a squeeze. "You're doing great, Henry. Almost there."

If I looked directly over the water, I could see Drummoyne

swimming pool and Terry Park, where Anika, Sean, and Melinda were waiting in the shade on blankets with cushions and baskets of food... exactly where I wanted to be.

"Only got the bridge to go."

I looked over at the Iron Cove Bridge, the bridge I'd driven over countless times, and noticed for the first time what connected the path to the bridge itself.

"Oh are you fucking kidding me? Stairs?"

Reed grinned. He fucking grinned. "Come on. You've got this, Henry."

By the time we got to the bottom of the stairs, I was mentally prepared to die. Reed waited at the first step with me, and together we looked up to the top. "It's just twenty steps."

It may as well have been twenty million.

"Tell me," Reed said. "When you first walked into the gym, on that very first day, how far could you run?"

"Not far."

"How many sit ups could you do?"

"None."

"How many steps could you do on the elliptical?"

"About ten."

"And how many can you do now?" he asked. "In just under two months, Henry, how far have you come?"

"A lot."

"Are you gonna let twenty steps stop you?"

I shook my head. "No."

"You've done over six kilometres, Henry. I'm telling you, you got this. You can do this."

I nodded. I could do this. Reed was right. I had come so far. With a deep breath, I did the sign of the cross, just in case, and took the first step. Then another, and another and another, and before I knew it, I was at the top, and I was on the home straight. I literally just had to run the length of the bridge, and it was all downhill from there.

I looked up at Reed. "I wanna run to the finish line."

His grin was breathtaking. "Atta boy."

So I gave it all I had. I left nothing behind, and I pushed myself harder. And when I thought I couldn't go another step, I just kept going.

I pushed and pushed and made the bridge, then the final few hundred metres back to where we started.

It almost killed me, but I fucking did it. I could barely stand, my legs were absolute jelly, my lungs were burning, and putting my hands on my knees and trying to breathe was all I could do to stop from keeling over.

Reed put his hands up, victory style. "You did it!"

I put my hand to my chest. "We." I took a few lungfuls of air. "We. Did. It."

"Henry!" Anika yelled, and I stood upright just before she collected me in a crushing hug. "You did it!"

"I did."

She let go of me like I was covered in some kind of contagious bacteria. "Oh my God, you're all sweaty." Then she was all excited from a safe distance. "But you did it!"

Some people walked past, and Anika announced to them, "He just did his first Bay Run!"

"Well done. Congratulations," they said.

I waved them off. "Trying. Not. To. Die."

Reed laughed and pulled me against him, kissing the side of my head. "You did it, Henry."

I let him hold me up. "Still trying not to die."

We turned to walk slowly back up to the picnic, where Sean and Melinda were waiting. Sean looked like he'd just woken up from a nap, and Melinda stood up and went to hug me, but when she saw me, she put her hands down and took a step back. "Oh. I'll hug you later. Well done, Henry."

"Great effort," Sean said.

"Thanks, guys." I collapsed onto the blanket, lying flat on my back. "Ugh. Everything hurts."

Reed sat down next to me. "You did great, Henry. I can't believe you ran the last part."

Anika cleared her throat. "Uh, excuse me. I ran from here all the way down to the path. Where's my gold medal?"

I snorted. "Stellar effort, Neeky."

"I know, right?" she said proudly. "Here, let me get you something to drink. You hungry?"

"I knew I brought you along for a reason."

She laughed and rifled through one of the picnic baskets, and I manoeuvred myself so I could rest my head on Reed's lap. "You right there?" he asked me.

"Still not entirely sure I'm not going to die," I explained.

He smiled down at me and pushed the hair off my forehead. "Can you believe you just did the Bay Run?"

"Nope. I wouldn't have done it without you."

His response was an eye-crinkling smile, which was my new favourite thing.

Anika held up a container. "Here's some grapes. And I have some crackers, some low-fat cheese."

"Low-fat cheese is a thing?" I asked.

"A disgusting thing," Anika said, "but a thing, nonetheless. I figured if you were doing this whole running thing, you wouldn't want normal food. I have apple juice, mineral water, and some filtered vitamin water or some such nonsense they're selling these days."

So we stayed at the park, lazing in the shade of the trees on blankets and snacking on fruits and crackers, talking and laughing for hours. It gave me a warm thrill to know my friends liked Reed and that he liked them. There would be no division, no separation in social circles, like there had been with Graham. Reed laughed with Sean and chatted with Anika and Melinda while I rested my head on his lap.

When I tried to sit up, my body protested, and I groaned. "Oh good Lord. Do the Bay Run, they said. It'll be fun, they said."

Anika sipped her juice. "They lied, honey."

Reed laughed and sprang to his feet. He held out his hand for me to hold so he could pull me up. "Let's get you home."

We helped pack up the picnic and said our farewells, with promises to talk soon. Anika gave my hand a squeeze, and the smile in her eyes told me she liked him. Her approval made me happier than it should have. "I'll call you later," I told her.

"Hopefully you'll be too busy," she said cheerfully. I wanted to kick her in the shin, and Reed thankfully pretended not to get what she meant. She just laughed at my horrified glare. "Love you, Henry."

I flipped her off, then waved goodbye to Melinda before Reed and I walked back down to my car.

After all the lead-up to today, it was hard to believe it was over. I was proud of myself for completing the Bay Run and thankful for Reed being with me every step of the way.

"Where to now?" I asked.

Reed looked over the top of my car at me. "Your place."

I grinned, and hope of what was to come flooded my belly. When we got to my place, I threw my keys on the table and let out a groan.

Reed looked concerned. "How are you feeling?"

"Sore, but not as bad as I thought, to be honest."

"Want me to run you a bath?"

"You'd do that for me?"

Reed gave me a shy smile. "Of course."

"Then I would love that."

He planted a soft, wet kiss on my lips, lingering just long enough for me to want more. For me to know there would be more. And I knew then that we'd take our relationship that one step further today. I knew we'd end up in bed, and I knew I'd have him inside me.

My blood warmed at the thought, my cock stirred, and I hummed.

He smiled knowingly and bit his lip as he walked away. Yep. I knew exactly what we'd be doing. *All* afternoon, with a bit of luck.

I was going to be sore tomorrow from running today, so at this point, it was a case of go hard or go home.

I heard the bath water start and smiled to myself. I could get used to being looked after like this. He was so attentive, so considerate, it made me want to be the same for him. "Want something to eat?" I called out.

He appeared in the hallway. "Sure. Um, can I grab a real quick shower while the bath is running? I'll just get changed back into these clothes, but I'm a bit gross."

"Of course! Towels are in the linen press behind you. I'll fix us something to eat." While he did that, I sliced some Turkish bread, then diced some tomatoes, Spanish onion, drizzled the mix with cold-pressed olive oil and a splash of balsamic vinegar. When I had it all done, a clean and fresh Reed stood behind me and kissed the back of my neck.

"How do you make everything so fancy?"

I turned in his arms. "I don't really. It's just bruschetta."

I scooped up some of the topping onto a piece of toasted bread and lifted it to his lips. He bit into it, closed his eyes, and moaned. "My God," he mumbled with his mouth full. "So good."

I made one for myself and had to agree, it was pretty good. Fresh, sweet and tart, and delicious. Oil ran down my fingers, and I quickly licked at it, sucking my finger into my mouth. Reed grunted quietly, and when I looked up, saw his eyes were darker. He pressed me against the kitchen counter, then without any effort at all, he hoisted me up so I was sitting on the countertop. He fit between my legs, and with his hands still on my arse, he pulled me to the edge. I was more his height this way, and pressed against him, I could feel his hard on against mine.

"Fuck," he whispered.

I nodded and spoke against his lips. "Yes. Later."

His gaze shot to mine, and his pupils blew out. "Are you sure, Henry?"

There was unwavering truth in my eyes. "Yes."

He put his fingers under my chin and kissed me, deeper this time. I slid my arms around his neck and moved a little closer to the edge of the countertop, needing to feel as much of him as possible. He wrapped his strong arms around me, and I kind of regretted agreeing to a bath...

I pulled away from him. "Shit, the bath."

He stepped back, his lips kiss-swollen and his erection tenting his running shorts. "I'll check it." His voice was gruff.

"No, I will." I slid off the counter. "You stay here and finish the bruschetta. I won't be in the bath long."

I left him to it, needing a second to clear my head. It also gave me some time in the bathroom to get myself ready for him. The muscle soak was heavenly, the douching not so much, but the anticipation was off the charts.

It was like my body knew what was about to happen.

I wondered what I should wear when I walked out. Was being naked and pre-lubed too presumptuous? I mean, it would save time...

Reluctantly, I pulled on some sweatpants, although I left off underwear. I threw on a T-shirt as an afterthought, and when I walked out, Reed had cleaned up the kitchen and was sitting nervously on the sofa. He looked me up and down, and when he noticed I'd gone commando, his gaze shot to mine.

I raised an eyebrow at him, half-daring, half-pleading, and he chuckled. "You are trouble." But he stood slowly and walked over to me. He took my hand and put my palm to his cheek. "Are you sure, Henry?"

I nodded. "I trust you."

He closed his eyes and kissed my palm, then without another word, he led me to my bedroom. He stopped at my bed and saw where I'd thrown a condom and new bottle of lube onto the bedcover. He looked at me and chuckled.

"What?" I blinked innocently. "Too much?"

"Just one condom?"

"There's a dozen in the top drawer. I bought a box during the week."

"Thank God." He kissed me with smiling lips, but it didn't take long before the kiss got serious. He pulled my shirt off by the hem and slid his huge hand under the elastic of my sweatpants, down over my arse.

He growled, and the sound made me whimper in his mouth. He broke the kiss and put his forehead to mine. His eyes were heavy-lidded, his lips wet. "Get on the bed. Face down."

I did as he instructed, his dominant tone setting every cell in my body on fire. Still with my sweatpants on, I lay face-down, spread my legs wide and raised my hips. He groaned and pulled his shirt over his head, and I watched in rapt awe as he slid his shorts off.

Oh, hell fucking yes.

Reed knelt on the bed and positioned himself between my legs. He ran his hands up the back of my thighs and over my arse, only to grip the waistband of my sweatpants and pull them down over my hips.

"Oh, Henry," he whispered, placing reverent kisses to each arsecheek.

I rolled my hips, my level of need rising higher and higher. He fisted the material and pulled them down my legs, leaving me spread and naked for him.

He slid his hands back up my legs, following each touch with a kiss. The contrast between his calloused hands and soft lips was heavenly. He gently spread my arsecheeks and tongued my arsehole, and I fisted the bedcovers and gasped.

Then he slipped his tongue inside me, and I thought I would come right there, and he did it again and again, taking me to new heights of pleasure and anticipation for what I needed most. "Reed, please."

I heard the pop of the lube bottle and, soon afterwards, felt cool liquid and blunt, thick fingers right where I needed him. I groaned as he breached me, pushing back to meet him. It was so good, and so welcome, but still not what I craved. His lips were at my shoulder. "You want it so bad."

"I do," I said with a frustrated moan. "I want your cock inside me."

His breath hitched, and he kissed my shoulder as he pulled his fingers out of me. "Roll over for me."

I manoeuvred onto my back and had one knee raised so my foot was flat on the bed. He was on his knees, skilfully rolling a condom down his cock before he crawled over to me on all fours. He licked my hard on, quickly taking me into his mouth. He sucked me hard and deep, quickly bringing me to the edge, but stopping before I finished.

I growled in frustration this time. "Reed. Fuck."

It seemed to be just what he wanted, because he hitched one of my legs over his shoulder and bent me in half, his cock positioned perfectly at my hole. "Is this what you want?"

I nodded, and he oh so slowly pressed into me. I gasped at the intrusion, he felt so much bigger than I thought he would. He let me breathe through it, though his nostrils flared with his self-control. "You okay?" he asked softly.

I nodded again. "God, yes."

He pushed further in and he put a hand to my face. "I want to see your eyes when I'm inside you."

His words made my cock jerk between us, and I needed to touch myself. I reached between us and wrapped my hand around my dick. Reed moaned and pulled out a little, only to slide back in, further this time, deeper and harder, rubbing my prostate with precision. My orgasm rocked through me like a bomb detonation, pleasure ripped through me, and Reed held onto me with strong hands as I came.

When I could open my eyes, he was looking at me with wonder and a little pride. He kissed me, hard, completely wrapping his arms around me, and only when every inch of him was buried in me, he started to thrust and fuck.

He owned me with his tongue, with his cock, with his whole body.

Then his thrusts became erratic, pushing deeper into me, and with a strangled cry, he came. Every muscle in his body was strained, taut, and I could feel his cock pulse inside me as he filled the condom.

He collapsed on top of me, and I drew lazy patterns on his back until his normal brain function returned. He pulled his face back a little, his cheeks flushed, his lips pink and swollen. "You okay?"

I swiped my thumb across his cheek. "So much better than okay."

He smiled, then chuckled, and buried his face back into my neck. "Jesus, Henry," he mumbled. "That was incredible."

I hummed my contentment. "Yes it was."

He pulled out of me slowly but stayed on top of me. "We should shower."

I nuzzled his jaw. "Later."

He pulled the covers over us and snuggled into me. "Maybe we could nap a little."

"Mmm, nap, shower, order Thai food, and more sex."

He smiled against my skin. "Perfect."

EPILOGUE

I STOOD IN A SEA OF OTHER CONTESTANTS, PUMPED and excited. I was a little nervous, but I'd trained for six months for this. My co-workers had only trained for about two months, well, since I'd suggested we enter a team in the City2Surf fun run to raise money for kids' cancer. They didn't object too much. Well, Melinda did. And I think she could have seriously plotted my death, but she was beside me, ready to run with me.

Reed was on my other side. When I'd said to him that my boss Lillian had been inspired by the Monday morning tea cook along thing and said we should incorporate more team building exercises, he showed me a flyer someone had dropped into the gym for the fun run.

So, not only did the gym have a team entered, but my office did too. I had shirts made that read *Actuaries Do it Better*, and there was eight of us all up running, Lillian included. I had to admit, I was kind of proud of myself.

I was fitter now than I was when I ran my first Bay Run last year. I would never have a body like Reed, and I was happy with that. I still had stretch marks. I was still a little soft around the middle. I would still eat cheesecake if I wanted it, and I would enjoy wine and coffee, because that's who I am. But I now wore men's medium sizes. I'd never be a small, but my body shape had completely changed: I was thinner yes, had some muscle definition too. But I was fitter, more flexible, my blood pressure was perfect, my blood sugar levels low, and my cholesterol levels were good. I was healthier than I had ever been.

Happier too.

Let me be clear about something. My contentment did not come from weight loss. It came from accepting myself, and that was something Reed had taught me to differentiate. It came from setting goals and accomplishing them, even when I thought I couldn't. It came from being able to look in a mirror and being happy with who I saw smiling back at me. I never realised just how invisible I'd been——how invisible I'd wanted to be——when I was at my biggest. How I'd used humour as a shield to defend myself before others could throw hurtful slurs at me. I mean, I was still funny——okay, let's face it, I'm hilarious, and we all know it——but now my jokes weren't used as weapons. And the fact Reed fell in love with me when I was at my heaviest, and loved me still, proved to me that he was what I'd thought all along.

Perfect.

Reed and I have been together for a year. He moved in with me two months ago when his lease was up for renewal, and it made sense given he spent so much time there anyway. It didn't come as a shock to anyone. We slotted into each other's lives seamlessly: his family loved me, and my mum and sister loved him too. He's even escorted my mum to the Nespresso café a few times to see if George Clooney ever showed up.

He never has.

We still worked out together. We started doing the Bay

Run once a month. I could run the full seven Ks now without stopping, and when we'd decided to do the City2Surf, we started doing the Bay Run every second weekend. Going from seven kilometres to fourteen was gonna be hard, but I was up for it.

We weren't out to break records or to even run competitively. We just wanted to finish and raise some money for sick kids. I doubted I'd be running the whole distance, but the fact I was even doing it at all was a pretty remarkable milestone.

So, while we would run it, most of my colleagues were walking purely for the fun of it, and so we were all starting together at the tail end of the field. Along with eighty thousand other entrants, we waited. And when the starting gun fired, Reed took my face in his hands and planted a kiss on my lips. "We got this."

And so we ran.

For fourteen fucking kilometres.

Well, I walked up Heartbreak Hill, because never in history has a hill been so aptly named. Then again, Kilimanjaro does start with *kill a man*...

"Come on, you can jog this," Reed urged.

I made it to the top of the hill and gripped my side, fending off a stitch. I'd just run almost seven kilometres already. The Bay Run is flat; the City2Surf is not. "No I can't. I left my Supergirl cape at home," I panted, and some guy behind me snorted. I shrugged. Reed was my Superman; I was his Supergirl. I had no problem with that.

"I hate hills. All of them," I said, taking a deep breath. "Whose ridiculous idea was it to put hills here?"

Reed chuckled. "I don't know, but they should be fired."

"Exactly."

"You wanna walk for a bit?"

I took another breath and felt rested enough to continue. "Nah. Let's keep going."

The second half was slower than the first, and Reed kept a check on the latest Fitbit I'd given him for Christmas. "If you wanna keep going for time, you can," I said to him. I was slowing him down, and no doubt the guys he worked with were probably already finished by now.

"No way," he said as he ran. "We start together, we finish together."

And it was when he said things like that, that I pushed myself. And by the time the finish line came into view, my feet hurt, my legs were moving on autopilot, and I left my lungs and the will to live somewhere along New South Head Road.

But then I noticed all his workmates waiting at the finish line. And Anika and Sean? What the hell? I didn't know they were coming to watch. In fact, Anika had said she'd rather give herself a skin graft with a spoon than to run with us.

Yet there she was, jumping up and down, cheering us on. I imagined the *Chariots of Fire* theme song playing and put my arms up as I ran over the finish line. On jelly legs I bent over, trying to breathe while trying not to die, when I realised no one had come over to me. I had expected Reed to clap me on the back or Anika to at least not touch me because of how sweaty I was, but I was alone.

I spun around and saw why.

All of Reed's workmates, Emily included, as well as Anika and Sean, stood in a row holding a huge banner sign with big black letters.

HENRY, I'LL RUN TO THE FINISH LINE WITH YOU ANY DAY.

And there was Reed, on bended knee holding a ring in his hand. "Marry me," he said.

. . .

IF ANYONE WAS PISSED about not being there to witness the most epic proposal ever, they needn't have worried. It was on the front page of the *Sun-Herald*, under the title "He Said Yes!"

Well, of course I did.

He was everything to me. He encouraged me; he challenged me. He was my Thor in public, my Loki in the bedroom. He was the perfect balance for me.

He was my true counterweight.

Like I said. Perfect.

cue Chariots of Fire music
~~The Finish Line~~

About the Author

N.R. Walker is an Australian author, who loves her genre of gay romance. She loves writing and spends far too much time doing it, but wouldn't have it any other way.

She is many things: a mother, a wife, a sister, a writer. She has pretty, pretty boys who live in her head, who don't let her sleep at night unless she gives them life with words.

She likes it when they do dirty, dirty things... but likes it even more when they fall in love. She used to think having people in her head talking to her was weird, until one day she happened across other writers who told her it was normal.

She's been writing ever since...

———

nrwalker.net

ALSO BY N.R. WALKER

Throwing Hearts

Pieces of You - Missing Pieces #1

Pieces of Me - Missing Pieces #2

Pieces of Us - Missing Pieces #3

Lacuna

Tic-Tac-Mistletoe

Bossy

Code Red

Dearest Milton James

Dearest Malachi Keogh

Christmas Wish List

Code Blue

Davo

The Kite

Learning Curve

Merry Christmas Cupid

To the Moon and Back

Second Chance at First Love

Outrun the Rain

Into the Tempest

Touch the Lightning

EWB - Enemies With Benefits

Holiday Heart Strings

Bloom

The Men from Echo Creek

Merry Christmas Cupid

To the Moon and Back

Second Chance at First Love

Outrun the Rain

Into the Tempest

Touch the Lightning

EWB

Holiday Heart Strings

Bloom

Series Collections:

Red Dirt Heart Series

Turning Point Series

Thomas Elkin Series

Spencer Cohen Series

Imago Series

Blind Faith Series

Missing Pieces Series

The Storm Boys Series

Free Reads:

Sixty Five Hours

Learning to Feel

His Grandfather's Watch (And The Story of Billy and Hale)

The Twelfth of Never (Blind Faith 3.5)

Twelve Days of Christmas (Sixty Five Hours Christmas)

Best of Both Worlds

TRANSLATED TITLES:

ITALIAN

Fiducia Cieca (Blind Faith)

Attraverso Questi Occhi (Through These Eyes)

Preso alla Sprovvista (Blindside)

Il giorno del Mai (Blind Faith 3.5)

Cuore di Terra Rossa Serie (Red Dirt Heart Series)

Natale di terra rossa (Red dirt Christmas)

Intervento di Retrofit (Elements of Retrofit)

A Chiare Linee (Clarity of Lines)

Senso D'appartenenza (Sense of Place)

Spencer Cohen Serie (including Yanni's Story)

Punto di non Ritorno (Point of No Return)

Punto di Rottura (Breaking Point)

Punto di Partenza (Starting Point)

Imago (Imago)

Imagines

Il desiderio di un soldato (A Soldier's Wish)

Scambiato (Switched)

Tallowwood

The Hate You Drink

Ho trovato te (Finders Keepers)

Cuori d'argilla (Throwing Hearts)

Galassie e Oceani (Galaxies and Oceans)

Il peso di tut (The Weight of it All)

Pieces of You - Missing Pieces 1

French

Confiance Aveugle (Blind Faith)

A travers ces yeux: Confiance Aveugle 2 (Through These Eyes)

Aveugle: Confiance Aveugle 3 (Blindside)

À Jamais (Blind Faith 3.5)

Cronin's Key Series

Au Coeur de Sutton Station (Red Dirt Heart)

Partir ou rester (Red Dirt Heart 2)

Faire Face (Red Dirt Heart 3)

Trouver sa Place (Red Dirt Heart 4)

Le Poids de Sentiments (The Weight of It All)

Un Noël à la sauce Henry (A Very Henry Christmas)

Une vie à Refaire (Switched)

Evolution (Evolved)

Galaxies & Océans

Qui Trouve, Garde (Finders Keepers)

Sens Dessus Dessous (Upside Down)

La Haine au Fond du Verre (The hate You Drink)

Tallowwood

Spencer Cohen Series

Thomas Elkin One

Lacuna

German

Flammende Erde (Red Dirt Heart)

Lodernde Erde (Red Dirt Heart 2)

Sengende Erde (Red Dirt Heart 3)

Ungezähmte Erde (Red Dirt Heart 4)

Vier Pfoten und ein bisschen Zufall (Finders Keepers)

Ein Kleines bisschen Versuchung (The Weight of It All)

Ein Kleines Bisschen Fur Immer (A Very Henry Christmas)

Weil Leibe uns immer Bliebt (Switched)

Drei Herzen eine Leibe (Three's Company)

Über uns die Sterne, zwischen uns die Liebe (Galaxies and Oceans)

Unnahbares Herz (Blind Faith 1)

Sehendes Herz (Blind Faith 2)

Hoffnungsvolles Herz (Blind Faith 3)

Verträumtes Herz (Blind Faith 3.5)

Thomas Elkin: Verlangen in neuem Design

Thomas Elkin: Leidenschaft in klaren

Thomas Elkin: Vertrauen in bester Lage

Traummann töpfern leicht gemacht (Throwing Hearts)

Sir

So Unendlich Viel Liebe (To the Moon and Back)

Thai

Sixty Five Hours (Thai translation)

Finders Keepers (Thai translation)

Spanish

Sesenta y Cinco Horas (Sixty Five Hours)

Los Doce Días de Navidad

CHINESE

Japanese

Bossy

Portuguese

Sessenta e Cinco Horas

Printed in Great Britain
by Amazon

44440177R00158